Bonham, Frank

Gimme an H, gimme an E, gimme an L, gimme a P

DATE	BORROWER'S NAME	Homeroom
OCT 9 1985	Kathleen K.	109
NOV 14 '85	Wendy [illegible]	109
[illegible]N 10 '86	Robyn Temple	101
OCT 29 '86	Crystal Moon	209
FEB 24 '88	[illegible] Kempf	204
OCT 23 '90	Danny A.	107
JAN 28 1994	Olivia Hutchinson	105

Gimme an H, Gimme an E, Gimme an L, Gimme a P

Also by Frank Bonham

DURANGO STREET

MYSTERY OF THE RED TIDE

MYSTERY IN LITTLE TOKYO

MYSTERY OF THE FAT CAT

THE NITTY GRITTY

COOL CAT

THE GHOST FRONT

THE VAGABUNDOS

VIVA CHICANO

THE GOLDEN BEES OF TULAMI

THE RASCALS FROM HASKELL'S GYM

THE MISSING PERSONS LEAGUE

DEVILHORN

CHIEF

FRIENDS OF THE LOONY LAKE MONSTER

A DREAM OF GHOSTS

BURMA RIFLES

HEY, BIG SPENDER

THE FOREVER FORMULA

Gimme an H, Gimme an E, Gimme an L, Gimme a P

Frank Bonham

Charles Scribner's Sons
New York

Library of Congress Cataloging in Publication Data

Bonham, Frank.
Gimme an H, gimme an E, gimme an L, gimme a P.

SUMMARY: A high school boy tries to help a beautiful, suicidal cheerleader whose emotional disturbances become increasingly more evident.
[1. Emotional problems—Fiction] I. Title.
PZ7.B6415Gi [Fic] 80-23926
ISBN 0-684-16717-4

This book published simultaneously in the United States of America and in Canada—Copyright under the Berne Convention

5 7 9 11 13 15 17 19 F/C 20 18 16 14 12 10 8 6 4

Printed in the United States of America

For Melody Martin.
What a beautiful name.
What a beautiful person.

1

It was 8:20 PM in Encinitas, on the foggy Southern California coast. In the den of the Furlong home, Dana Furlong was reviewing with frustration a biology report on which he had received nine points out of a possible ten. His lab partner had scored twelve, on the identical worm dissection! What this proved was that his partner was exceptionally pretty, and that Mr. Lockwood, the teacher, gave girls all the breaks. Dana slapped the paper against the desk, grimaced, and looked at the clock.

A series of glutinous sounds caused him to glance around in annoyance. On the sofa, his younger sister was eating a red licorice whip and whispering Spanish to herself from a textbook. Chomp, chomp, whisper, whisper. Her Princess telephone rested on the floor at her feet, its long cord trailing down the hall to her room, like a clue in a treasure hunt. Her following him around the house should not have bothered him, but it had begun to. She had been parking herself near him to eat and do her homework for years, but recently the sound track of her presence had begun to irritate him.

In exasperation, he said, "Ahem!" When Wendy did not react, he cleared his throat and said, "I know you're busy, Sis, but so am I. Do you have to work in here?"

Wendy, twelve, looked at him in surprise. "I guess not. Do you?"

"I was here first, kiddo, and I'm going to make a call in a few minutes. I'm sorry, but I don't want to be interrupted."

"I won't interrupt you. So what's the problem?"

"One problem is the noise you make muttering conjugations with your braces glued together. The other is that you might get a call while I'm making mine."

Wendy grinned. Red threads of candy were woven through the thousand-dollar barbed-wire entanglement over her front teeth. "Hey, neat!" she said, laughing. "Then we can trade, if we get bored with our own calls. Laura kind of gets wound up sometimes."

"Yes, doesn't she."

"Who are you calling?"

"Whom. It's a business call. And if I hear you popping that gumbo while I'm trying to talk, I won't help you with your subjunctives."

"I'll be quiet," Wendy promised. "What's the call about?"

"I'm answering an ad for lovebirds."

"You answered one last week."

"Oh, is there a quota?" Dana said, in a sneering way; and then frowned at his sarcasm, which was new to him, too. Maybe his lab partner was getting to him with her twelves, and her teasing. . . .

"Why are you buying more birds?" Wendy asked. "You'd have to build another aviary, wouldn't you?"

"No. I could move some young birds around. This would be a fantastic bargain, and I've at least got to make a pass at the field."

Dana raised the offensive lab write-up and shook it like a naughty kitten. "Want to know how to get straight A's in biology?" he asked.

" 'Kay."

"Take art courses, and use eyeliner. My lab partner and I dissected a worm last week. I got a B on my write-up, and she—with exactly the same data!—got an A+. She may do beautiful drawings, but what's that got to do with worms? In fact, I was the one who discovered that what she identified as lungs were seminal vesicles. Lungs in a worm! Ever hear a worm pant?"

Wendy looked intrigued. "Is she that cheerleader you mentioned?"

"Katie Norman, yes."

Looking thoughtful, Wendy stretched another red whip until it recoiled against her teeth like a serpent. "Did she do that caricature of you on the back of your report? I was looking at it. It's cute. I noticed it has her initials."

Dana scoffed. "Cute! It's lousy. Do I chew my lip that way when I'm reading? No way."

Wendy laughed. "Ha! You gnaw on it like a pork chop."

Dana experimentally nibbled his lip, and frowned. "Really? Hmmm. Well, trust Katie N. to pick up on it."

His attempt to sound scornful did not fool her. Her eyes gleamed as she watched him try to sneer. For between him and the little cheerleader there was some blind attraction against which they were both struggling. When they were together, they took digs at one another. Though Katie N. was neat in person, she was as sloppy as a fry-cook in her lab work, and he could not resist suggesting better ways of doing things. Then she got an A+ and he got a B! It made him look like a conceited twit.

In fact, since she had transferred to Santo Tomas High at mid-term, he had begun secretly to worry about himself. Nothing serious, but she had let some little mice of self-doubt loose to run about his attic. She accused him of being as set in his ways as an old man. Well—maybe he was stolid; but he always had been, so why had it never bothered him before?

He realized Wendy had said something to him.

"What's that?"

"I said, are you going to ask her for a date?"

"Are you kidding? I've only known her a few months."

"Some guys would have proposed by now. Are you going to ask her?"

"No!"

"But you like her, don't you?" Wendy forged on.

"Not really. Besides, I don't have time for birds and girls, both. It's one or the other. Be quiet, now," he warned, drawing the desk phone toward him.

"What's the deal?"

"Somebody's selling black-masked lovebirds for ten dollars apiece. That's fantastic—the going price is forty! So I'm going to find out what's going on. Could be a distress sale—new breeder —something like that."

Wendy nibbled the tip of another licorice whip. "Wasn't that ad last week a freaky price, too?"

"Right. Blue-masked lovebirds. But I called too late, and they were all sold."

The advertiser the week before had been a young woman who spoke English with a Spanish accent. She was Colombian, she told him. Maybe she had smuggled in the birds she was selling, since the price was so far below market. But she had sounded nice; rather sexy, in fact.

He started to punch the numbers into the

phone, but muttered and started over. He had hit a two for a three. His mind had still been on Katie Norman, but now he firmly evicted her from his thoughts, like closing the door on an obstinate sales person. The telephone played him a little tune as he composed the numbers; he frowned at its familiarity. Had he dialed it before? Odd . . .

2

At the breakfast bar, the Lantz children were still devouring ice cream, though it was past their bedtime. Katie Norman sat erect, trance-like, in the big leather television chair with her eyes closed and the sound turned low on a police program. In her mind a terrifying life-or-death drama was being enacted to which she was a horrified, yet consenting, witness. The shrieking of police tires on the tube had started it. She had sworn to abstain from fantasy until after the children were in bed. These daydreams had become her drug of choice, and like any narcotic they were proving to be cruel masters. But once again she had succumbed. Behind her eyelids her eyes moved rapidly back and forth, like those of a sleeper in the REM phase.

. . . The driver of the sports car was only sixteen, and her blond hair fluttered like the ribbons of the pompons on the seat beside her. With her blue eyes uptilted at the outer corners, and her heart-shaped face and tempting lips, she was the picture of a teen-

age fashion model. She wore a white sweater, a blue-and-white cheerleader's skirt, and white shoes. She had driven to the mountains straight from pep-squad practice. There was a tiny blemish on her right cheek—an amoeba-shaped birthmark. It would make identification easier.

The girl was driving down the Palomar Observatory grade like a maniac.

"Katie!" Herbie Lantz's voice cried. "Wake up!"

A sign at the top of the grade had advised motorists to exercise caution on the hairpin curves. But the girl in the candy-apple Porsche was blasting along on the edge of disaster, the car's engine howling, a near vertical drop on the right, a rocky cliff on the left. At every turn the rear wheel would chew out into the gravel and dust would fly, but she would bring the car back like an experienced—

"Katie! Katie!" Herbie and his sister chanted.

But suddenly the blond driver was out of control! The car was plunging down the slope to where the road doubled back after another tight curve. Katie saw herself flung clear, landing like a doll on the blacktop. On the grimy roadbed, her hair shone like a swatch of gold lamé.

Within minutes, disaster sightseers and rescue workers were gathering. A young doctor knelt beside the girl's body. Although Katie knew she was dead, she was somehow aware of everything that went on. To her surprise, she saw a yellow moped pull up, and the boy from her biology lab jumped off it and hurried up to a helmeted highway patrolman.

"Officer, I know her!" he babbled. "She's a cheerleader at my school. Will she—be alright?" His name was Dana Furlong, and though he was a very bright boy, he sometimes used his cleverness to hurt people.

"Throw water on her!" Herbie cried. "That's what they do to wake people up!" But though Katie struggled to respond, she could not force her eyelids open.

The young doctor walked to where Dana stood with the policeman. "There's not a mark on her body," he declared, puzzled. "And yet her heart has stopped beating."

"That's terrible!" Dana groaned. "She was the most beautiful girl at Santo Tomas High. She was my lab partner in biology. Gee, I hope this didn't have anything to do with the way I treated her. I used to be kind of picky when we'd do a dissection—make her take the notes while I did the work, or criticize her when she cut up the worm. Maybe she was—lonely, or something. . . ."

The cop patted his shoulder. "A cheerleader lonely? No way."

Then, standing beside Dana, Katie saw a young woman who was always present in her reveries. Her features resembled Katie's, but she was older, in her twenties, and wore a granny gown and a tapestry headband. She looked like a protestor from the sixties.

"Don't blame yourself, Dana," she said. "Were

you her friend? I'm her real mother. I shouldn't have left her alone so much. I'll have to live with this forever. . . ."

Katie tried to rouse herself—the self lying broken on the blacktop. "Mama!" she cried. But the woman did not seem to hear her, and Katie realized her body still lay motionless. She struggled again to attract her mother's attention. "I'm right here, Mama! I'm alright—!"

Now the children were tugging at her hands, and Katie opened her eyes and took a deep, shaky breath. Dazed and still in shock, she stared at the kids, who appeared to be imitations of children. Were they real, or were the people on the Palomar grade real? But then a little relay in her head clicked, and the parts of the puzzle assembled themselves as if magnetically. She was alive; she was at the Lantz's; the kids were real, and demanding attention. She gave a shiver, but managed to smile.

Herbie Lantz—this was the first time Katie had baby-sat him and his sister—was jumping up and down before her, waving his arms. He was wearing a white plastic mixing bowl on his head.

"Look—I'm doing a hurkie!" he screeched.

Katie got up, dazed but laughing. "No, that's not the way," she said.

She went into one of her pep routines, neat and feminine and perky. "Hey, gimme a blue! Hey, gimme a white! And gimme a team, fight-fight!"

she chanted, clapping. "Yay, blue, yay, white, yay, team, fight, fight!"

The children yelled and clapped. "Do another, do another!"

"Next time," Katie said. "Get into your p.j.'s now. Woops, there's the telephone again."

"It's rung twenty times tonight!"

"Six," Katie said. The children ran off to the bedroom wing, and she picked up the telephone on the table. She pushed the hair from her ear and snuggled the receiver in place.

"The Lantz residence," she said.

"Did you run an ad about lovebirds?" a man's voice asked. He sounded like a night watchman, gruff and suspicious.

"Yes, but they're all sold."

She hung up. That was the only way to handle bird people, she had found. With any encouragement, they gabbled on and on, about their birds, their grandchildren, their late husbands or wives. Dana Furlong was the only one she had talked with who wasn't a total clod.

She tucked Mary, five, in bed first, and dimmed the light. As she bent down to kiss her, the little girl reared up like a ghost and threw her arms around Katie's neck, giggling. Katie squirmed.

"Hey, settle down," she said.

"Tell me a secret! You promised."

"Alright. But don't tell anybody. It's about a boy named Dana. He likes me, but he hasn't decided to let me know yet. So I'm keeping it a secret, too. Isn't that weird?"

"How can you tell he likes you?"

"That's *next* week's secret! 'Night!"

She made sure Herbie was properly tucked between the sheets and turned out the light. As she pecked his sticky cheek, he whispered, emboldened by the darkness, "You're pretty, Katie."

"Thank you. Go to sleep, now."

The telephone was ringing again, but she stopped in the bathroom to regard herself dubiously in the mirror. Pretty? Pretty as a pimple. For, as usual, she saw the tiny birthmark first. And in despair she realized that her features were as blank as a wig block. And her eyes! Like tiny stones in a dime-store ring. Pretty? Oh, Herbie! I guess I *was* pretty at twelve, but Daddy's pretty little doll has matured into a klutz.

The telephone stopped ringing, as another bird person gave up. The Lantzes had said they'd check with her at nine, and Dana Furlong, being such a dynamite science major—when he had to underline something he used a ruler!—would call at exactly the time mentioned in the ad. He had been five minutes late last week, however, to her surprise.

It was 8:29 when she went back to the family room. As she entered, the telephone rang.

She took her time getting comfortable, snuggled

the receiver sensuously against her ear, and said, *"Bon soir."*

"Um—" It was Dana's voice, and he had been thrown off by her French. "Did you advertise some birds for sale?"

"Comment?" she said. "Wat you say?"

"Are the girl—um, person—who advertised black-masked lovebirds?"

"Ah, beards! *Oui!* Zee you letter." Fantastic! He had no idea it was she.

"Wait! Are they sold?" Such anguish in his voice!

"You espeak French?" she asked.

"No. Well, just a little. I'm taking it, but—*un tout petit pou."*

"Peu," she corrected. "Well, I haf to tell you somesing. Zey are sold."

"Sold," he said. "Damn—sorry, *mademoiselle. Je regrette."*

"Ah, you spik very good French!" Katie cooed.

"Good night," the boy said.

"But I dawn unnerstan'," Katie said. "Don't you een'erested in beards?"

"Yes, but if they're sold—"

"Uh-huh, all sold. But mos' beard people lak to talk about beards."

"Birds," Dana corrected. "By the way, *mademoiselle,* who are you? Do you live here?"

"Not talk zo fest, please. I inhabit at Paris,

assist—how you say?—wait at Sorbonne school. Go. Attend. I come to visit frands. But oh, la, la! I buy so many sings! And now I am going home, and I mus' sell all zese beards I buy. You comprehend?"

"I guess. You go to the Sorbonne, huh? College girl?"

"Uh-huh, girl. No boy. Ooney-vair-seetay. I drive race cars, *aussi.*"

"Oh, yeah?"

"*Ah, oui.* At Le Mans."

"But I thought only men—"

"Spashul case. Because I win—won, am winning—at Grand Prix. What you do, *mon ami?*"

"I go to high school. As a hobby, I raise beards."

"*Ah, mon ami,*" Katie reproved, sadly, "you make fun wiz me."

"No, I'm just disappointed about the birds. You mean you sold thirty black-masked lovebirds for ten dollars apiece? Lady, you just lost about thirty bucks—dollars—apiece on them, or roughly nine hundred dollars."

"*Ah, mon dieu!* But I ask ze man at ze wholesale farm, how much zese beards worse? He say, Oh, not zo much. Zere is so many of zem for sale jos' now. *Mon Dieu!* Zat man is so bad!"

"Tough. Well, good night, *mademoiselle.* Hey, you didn't tell me your name."

"Anne-Marie. How you call yourself, *monsieur?*"

"Dana. You're not the girl—young woman—who advertised beards laz wik—excuse me!—birds last week? No, I guess she was from Colombia. She had a slight accent, too."

"*Non, monsieur,* I just come zis place."

"I see. Hmm. Well, good night, *mademoiselle.*"

"You een a hurry, *garcon?*"

"I've got a little homework. *Devoir, non?*"

He did not wait to hear whether *devoir* meant homework: he hung up. She wrinkled her nose, but blew the telephone a kiss. I love him, I hate him; he loves me, he loves me not. Then her eyes misted and she sniffled a little.

You think I'm mean, don't you? I heard you say something contemptuous about me to Paul Quinn one day. Just because I left you with your mouth hanging open to go talk to the jocks. But popularity's my major, Dana: Three units. Lab course.

Won't you ever get the point? I wouldn't tease you if I didn't like you. And I've got to have some help—and pretty darned soon, or they'll get inside my skull, see what's going on there, and lock me up with a lot of smelly old retards. Forever! Katie the career basket-maker; Katie the graying painter-by-the-numbers.

That's why I can't tell anybody but you about my fantasies. And not even you, until you understand that I'm not really a loony. You'd be scared off if I spilled all this stuff that's driving me crazy, in this chop suey I call my brain. I've got to wait for the right time; and that depends on you.

But don't talk to me about shrinks!

Do you know what they did to Ernest Hemingway? They gave him electroshock, day after day, cremated his memory and turned his brain to pudding. He tried to escape, but they kept dragging him back, taping electrodes to his head, and throwing the switch.

They put a towel in your mouth so you won't bite your tongue off when you go into convulsions. You wet your pants and soil yourself. Did you read *Cuckoo's Nest?* Well, that's what they do to you.

But they won't do it to me! Because I'm not telling anybody about what's going on in my head. Anybody!

Katie's fists clenched and she squeezed her eyes shut. Someone inside her head was screaming like a mad girl. I'm not a loony, Dana! she tried to say over the shrieking. But I've got these terrible problems to solve! You think calculus is hard?

Suppose that A = me, simple, uncomplicated little cheerleader. But X = Marcia, and Y = Daddy, and Z = Cutepig. Still with me? But the whole mess is divided by my real mother, who is expressed as $\frac{AX}{Y} \div Z$, so that if I try to please Marcia, I see Mom standing there jeering at me for letting such a square run my life.

And what about Daddy? If he loves Marcia, how can he love me? He must know she and I despise each other. But as bad as she is, she hasn't dumped me like Mom did. Mom, you wimp! I was only *nine*, for Pete's sake!

Oh, shut up! she screamed at the idiot girl babbling in her head. Take your problems and stuff them! You think too much. Your mirror gets sick of looking at you. Ah, but know something? I could kill you, and Marcia, and the whole bunch of you, easy. There are some pills in Marcia's medicine chest . . . Or I could take the keys to her car and play the Palomar grade game. And we'd all go to sleep like children, and . . .

As she calmed down, she was surprised to discover that she was gasping. She was shocked by the intensity of her feelings. I've really got to do something about myself before somebody else does, she realized.

So I thought I'd talk to you, Dana. You were supposed to have found me by now—gotten mad about the ads, found the address, and come storming in looking for the bird girl who's been teasing you and wrecking your bird market. And there she would be! Your lab partner and girlfriend—the culprit! And you'd have sensed in a flash that I wouldn't have done it if I hadn't loved and trusted you, and wanted your help.

But you'd better find me pretty soon; because I'll tell you, genius, sometimes dying makes a lot more sense than living. It would be just like sleeping. One long happy dream.

Oh, boy.

Katie discovered she had been weeping. She went into the bathroom and washed her face, bathed her eyes so they would be less red from crying. Then she went back and lifted the receiver from the cradle so that she could do her homework without all those idiotic bird people hounding her. (What's a smart boy like you doing in the bird world, Dana?) She opened her notebook, on which she had painted a small horse and the words: MUSTANGS, Yay! English III, Amanda Allen.

"Assignment: Write a parody of a nineteenth century poet, any subject."

Katie flipped through an anthology, looking for short poems. Aha! "My Garden," by Thomas Edward Brown. She scribbled for about ten minutes, then closed the notebook. Over to you, Amanda! Worry your head over *that* one!

Mrs. Allen was not only an English teacher, but also a counselor for disturbed students; certainly, in fact, the port of embarkation for the loony bin.

It was almost time for the Lantzes to call. But she had one more thing to take care of. To make sure there was no one around, she peered out the front window. The street was foggy and silent, a street lamp standing like a lighthouse in the mist. It would not have surprised her to see a fishing boat with green running lights go gliding by.

She carried her purse into the children's bathroom, locked the door, and extracted a flexible plastic tube about six inches long. She squeezed it flat and pressed one end against the side of her throat, about where a boy usually sucked on a girl's neck to create a hickie. She drew on it, hard. By moving it several times, she was able to create the illusion of a hickie implanted on her flesh by some impassioned boy. It drove Marcia nuts, wondering who was giving her the hickies.

She had just replaced the telephone handset on its cradle when it began to ring. Katie picked it up, smiling.

"Oh, yes, Mrs. Lantz—everything's fine! No, no trouble. I'm sorry about that, but I had a zillion weird calls about birds, so I took it off the cradle. Did you advertise some lovebirds for sale? Well, I didn't *think* so, but they kept calling.

"Anyway, the children were super, and I'm teaching them some cheerleading routines. . . . Oh, you were? Hey, that's neat. My real mother was a cheerleader, too. I don't know," she giggled, "maybe she still is. I haven't seen her for years. . . ."

3

At breakfast the next morning, a vision of Katie Norman kept dodging like a gnat before Dana's eyes. He had been brooding over the peculiar conversation with the French bird girl, but the face of Katie continued to intrude. Finally he realized why: The cheerleader on the cereal box closely resembled Katie, both of them pretty, blond, and full of pep—and probably no deeper than their nail polish. Pep squad types.

Then he saw with annoyance that Wendy was eating her favorite breakfast food, Bran Bubbles ("You Can Hear The Goodness"). Dana could definitely hear *something* as she chewed, but it sounded more like horsefeed than goodness.

"Don't eat that garbage," he said in despair. "I've told you about nutrition. There's more food value in paper matches than in that stuff you're eating. What's wrong with the mixture I make?"

Wendy grinned, looking up from her magazine. "Good question."

"'If I fed my birds the way you eat, their feathers would fall out. So will yours.'"

Outside the kitchen door the shrill chattering of lovebirds went on without pause. The patio aviary was enclosed by a green jungle of subtropical plants that formed the side boundary of the lot. The fog last night had left all the green leaves dripping. Aviaries were squeezed into every nook and cranny of the garden.

Dana filled a bowl with Furlong's Formula, a cereal blend he had worked out with a dietitian and his father's computer. He added milk and, as he ate, skimmed the classified ads in the morning paper. In the dining room, he heard his mother, in bathrobe and hair curlers, shuffling up another hand of bridge.

"Did you call about those birds last night?" she asked.

"Yes. Another fruitcake ad. The last one was a young woman from Colombia who was settling her aunt's estate—some famous aviculturist I never heard of. This was a spendthrift from France. But black-masked lovebirds for ten bucks apiece? Not very likely."

"Two no trump," his mother muttered. "Three clubs—"

"What?" Dana asked.

"Did I say something?"

Dana rolled his eyes at Wendy, who snickered. Bridge from morning till night. Bridge weekends.

Bridge camps and lessons. Master points. Black to move and win. No, no—that was chess.

"I'm sorry, dear—lovebirds?" their mother said. "How much should the birds have cost?"

"At least forty. *Hey, listen to this!*" He had developed an intuition for the bird ads, his mind rejecting the daily notices for food supplements, cages, and pet shops, and homing in on the new ads.

MUST SELL: Six proven pairs cherryheads,
$50 a pair.
Call after 8:30 PM. *768–0901.*

"Okay!" he said fiercely, tearing the ad from the paper. "Aha! That gives me a handle. Nobody but this loony says 'must sell' and 'after 8:30 PM,' so it's got to be her again. The same psycho."

"Were the telephone numbers all the same?" asked Wendy.

"No, but haven't we got three numbers ourselves? Your phone, Dad's WATS line, and 0339. So that's no big mystery. And the ad says 'cherryheads.' That word has been out of style for years—we say 'yellow,' now—so she's getting her lingo out of old bird magazines. Plus, nobody in his right mind would sell yellows for less than two hundred a pair; three hundred would be more like it for proven pairs.

"What do you think?" Dana called to his mother.

"Darn," she said, vexed over a card she had just turned up. Then, "Hmm? It beats me, dear. By the way," her voice becoming disciplinary, "Dad was asking how you're doing in calculus lately. . . ."

Dana yawned. He was irritated that it was so hard to break through the Great Bridge Wall to her reasonably good mind. And he wanted to discuss this mystery with someone with an objective point of view. He knew that his own opinion was colored slightly by the intriguing, possibly sexy, quality of the bird girl's voice.

"Oh, did Daddy call?" he said, with a wink at Wendy. "Where is he? In Houston with the biochemists, or in San Francisco with the cryobiologists?"

"In Houston. He made the point that you're not going very far in science without a solid background in math."

Dana crushed a Bran Bubble and wrinkled his nose at the brown dust, which resembled mummy powder. "If you think I'm bad in math, you should see some of my work in biology. I try, Lord, Lord, but—"

"Nonsense! It's a natural for you. Ever since you were a little boy you've loved bugs—and of course birds. Like father, like son—"

"It's amazing," Dana said, surprised at his own bitterness this morning, "how much we're alike. He's six feet one, I'm five-eight. He's blond, I'm dark. He does bridge problems, I count the barbs in lovebird feathers. What could be more natural than for me to stumble along in his famous footsteps?"

"Fiddlesticks," his mother muttered. She was looking at a card, in disappointment. For a moment he had thought she was going to comment on his unlikely career in biochemistry. What was likely—almost certain—was that he would end up in a windowless lab somewhere peering through a microscope all his life, the aging technician.

He gave up on his mother as an idea-source and began doodling with a calculator he carried on his belt, a marvel no larger than a business card, but capable of wonders a ten-ton computer of a generation ago could not have achieved.

Start from scratch.

Suppose the cherryheads really existed.

Assume that he bought all six pairs for three hundred dollars. On a simple resale of the birds, at the market price, he could make nearly a thousand!

But he didn't have three hundred.

What he did have was friends with a little money. Paul Quinn, his closest friend, almost supported himself on audio work, from friends and custom stereo shops. Count on Paul for a hundred.

Ruben Lara made surfboards. He should be good for fifty.

Francis Goodman, editor of the school paper, had an allowance, and might raise fifty. Dana would come in with the final hundred.

He'd let the six pairs reproduce once, getting at least eighteen babies worth a hundred apiece. Wow! He sat back, breathless.

What it came down to was the probability that on the single phone call he was going to make tonight, the consortium could net twenty-seven hundred dollars!

If the seller really existed.

If he/she actually had any birds.

But how could the ads not be genuine? It cost nearly ten dollars to run a two-line ad. Ten dollars to talk to strangers? Ridiculous. Probably he'd called too late both times.

So, joke or not, he would be foolish not to make the call.

4

Dana placed four flat bowls of halved apples and chopped greens on a bench outside the kitchen door. His prize aviary was at the far end of the roofed patio, its front wall forming a screen partially shrouded by shade plants. A dozen miniature parrots of various colors went about their business of eating, preening, and cutting up palm-fronds with their beaks. In the morning sunlight they dodged like beams in a laser show, blue, green, yellow, coral.

He did not see the particular bird he was looking for, his Million-Dollar Baby.

Carrying a bowl, he slipped into the aviary. The birds collected on a perch to chatter at him. The blue hen was in a nest box with her single baby. She had laid five eggs eight weeks ago, but only one had been fertile. The tiny blob of pink silly-putty that emerged had now developed into a husky little mutant as big as its mother.

He placed the blue hen's nest box on a shelf and raised the lid. The hen emerged, chattering angrily, and joined the other birds to gossip about him. He probed among the dried palm fibers and found the warm body of the baby. It clung to the nesting material as he extracted it, like a nut from a shell. He smiled in pleasure at its perfection.

It was an albino, a rarity, greenish-white except for the ebony band of immaturity across its horn-colored beak. Its eyes were as red as garnet. He talked to it, examined it, felt it warm in his hand. It was the next-to-the-last step in his struggle to develop a true blue peachface, a first. Furlong's Peachface!

With a little bit of luck.

His genetic charts said it could be done. Many breeders were trying, but no one had succeeded. There were rumors of a true blue in Holland. A breeder in England said no, it was more of a peacock blue. The goal was a light blue bird, a clear azure.

His own genetic chart promised that in the next generation he could expect twenty-five percent blues. In this small white parrot's body there were already the genes of the bird with which he was going to surprise the bird world.

He finished feeding the birds, placed his books in a green backpack, and headed for school on his moped, bought with profits from his bird business.

Lab today. His heart did a happy little movement like a lovebird luxuriously stretching out a wing. It was his turn to dissect and Katie's turn to take the notes. He would work into the conversation the money he was going to make on the cherryhead buy. (But don't make a fool of yourself, he thought. Don't let it sound like you're bragging. Bring it in smoothly, like, "Speaking of dead cats, Katie, I'm going to make twenty-seven hundred bucks on a lovebird transaction.")

Furlong, you'll do it, too, he knew! And be sorry later. You and your lovesick mouth. Why do you keep trying to impress her? Who is she? A brighter-than-average cheerleader. So why do you care what she says and does?

Unfortunately, he did.

5

Dana chained his moped to the bike rack, next to another belonging to his friend, Paul Quinn. He slung the tote bag over his shoulder and climbed the steps from the parking lot to the arched entrance of the school complex. It resembled the portal of an honor camp, ugly and no-nonsense. But from the stuccoed archway you could gaze back over avocado groves on the hillsides below, across homes, eucalyptus trees, and palms to the Pacific Ocean, a half-mile west. Suddenly, as he stood there, a little red Porsche convertible, gleaming like a waxed Delicious apple, came at a rush into the parking lot and halted with a gritty skid. The woman driver's voice, raised to carry over the wind and engine noise, came clearly from the car. It had the harsh quality of that of a talking parrot.

". . . Clean up your act, sweetheart, or go on house arrest again. . . . By eleven next time, or else . . ."

The voice faded as the driver, an attractive young woman in a ski cap, saw Dana and stared at him with hostility. Beside her sat Katie Norman! She was wearing a little brown hat that turned up all around. She got out, neat and trim in brown slacks and a short-sleeved red sweater over long white sleeves with frilled cuffs. The woman made a final waspish statement to Katie, which cause the girl to shrug, and then the woman drove off.

Katie looked up and saw Dana. She smiled, wiggled her fingers at him, and trotted up the steps.

"Hi, Cheers," Dana said, twanging with excitement.

"Hi, Kapitan."

"Kapitan! How come you always call me that?"

"Because you're so organized. Up 'scope! Down 'scope! Proceed at full speed. Fire one, fire two. Yawn on the green light."

"Actually, they say 'flank speed,' " Dana noted, defensively. But he rallied, with a grin. "What was that about house arrest?"

Katie glanced at him, startled. There was a two-second meeting of their eyes, hers worried, his surprised. For an instant she looked vulnerable, almost frightened. Then she laughed, not very convincingly.

"Oh, you heard it? Little family joke."

Joke? he thought. The driver—her sister?—had appeared dead serious.

"Did you stay out too late?" he asked.

"*Forget* it, Kapitan," she said impatiently. "I said it was a family joke. Take all day to explain."

"Okay! Sorry."

And once again they were squaring off in slightly disappointed silence. They trailed through a labyrinth of small courtyards and one-story buildings like barracks. Santo Tomas was not really a large school, but a large collection of small schools, add-on appended to add-on for thirty years. Katie kept greeting people with squeals of pep squad vigor.

Then she thought of something else to bug him with. "What did you get on the worm dissection? I got twelve out of ten!"

Dana cleared his throat. "So I heard. I got nine. My lousy drawings, I guess. Anyway, Lunkhead likes girls."

"Mr. Lockwood's neat. I like his sense of humor."

"Yeah, I hear Bluebeard was a barrel of laughs, too."

"Well, it's your own fault if he gives you a hard time. Why do you keep bugging him?"

"I don't 'bug' him, Katie. I just correct the worst of his errors. I'm trying to educate him. Beneath the ragged fur of this beast there may lie a lovable clod."

Katie trilled a canarylike laugh. "And you

wonder why I get twelves and you get nines! —Hi, Annie! See you in English!"

Another courtyard, another cloister. A congregation of athletes grouped along Stud Wall saw Katie and began howling. "Awright, men! Don't waste your time on that science major, Katie! Come here, chick!"

Dana had just said, "I had a funny experience last night," when she ran over to join the jocks. He grimaced, told himself angrily, Forget her! But the sad fact was that once again she had left him standing with the wrong map at a fork in the road.

6

Four boys were talking before the biology bungalow when Dana arrived. Two of them, science majors like himself, had calculators clipped to their belts. He heard Francis Goodman orating; Francis was the editor of the school paper.

"Jocks! Surfers! Thespians! You need a passport to migrate from one part of the campus to another. In ancient Greece—"

"In Greece, Francis, they had sour wine to unify them," Paul Quinn said. "Specialization has polarized us. Maybe for the better."

Ruben grinned at Dana. "Where's Katie?" he said. "I thought I saw you with her."

"Katie had a yell to lead," Dana said. He had been full of zest for his bird consortium; but now he had to pump himself up like a bicycle tire. "Have I got a deal!" he said, groping in his notebook for the newspaper clipping. "There was an ad this morning—"

"Don't take it personally," Paul interrupted.

"What? The ad?"

"No . . . Katie. Cheerleaders are specialists,

too. Knowing the jocks is part of their work. I get the same from Annie, my thespian lady. She's been talking about her professional obligation to date Charlie Harris, the famous actor and senior. Do I resent it? God, Dana, I could kill him."

"She's just practicing what you preach," Francis said, innocently. "She can learn things from Charlie that she can't from you."

"Telling me?" Paul sighed. He was the cliché genius, with a long, famished frame, uncombed hair, and horn-rimmed glasses.

"Stick around a minute," Dana muttered, as Ruben showed signs of moving off to join the surfing clique down the quad. When he dallied with the science clique, it was to pick their brains for technical information on the hydraulics of a new board.

Dana waved the column he had torn from the paper. "You're looking opportunity right in the teeth. Would you believe nine hundred percent profit in six months?" He explained how, with a small initial investment and twenty dollars worth of birdseed and spinach, they could make a killing.

"Ever hear of smuggled birds?" Paul asked, amused.

"Smuggled birds are usually Mexican parrots. These are African lovebirds, probably domestic. They'd have numbered legbands, which I'd check with the Lovebird Society."

"It's a joke, Dana," Ruben said. "Some girl's playing a practical joke."

"A joke? When I run an ad it costs me eight-eighty for two lines. Some girl's going to pay that much just to play a joke? It won't cost anything to look into it. But if we buy them, I'll need cash—a hundred from you, Paul; fifty from you, Ruben; and—"

"Oh, Dana, this is getting serious," a girl called from the doorway to the lab. "Birds again? You should be attending an aviary, not a high school."

It was Katie, laughing as she strolled toward them. Dana saw that she had put on lipstick and a little blue eyeshadow since she left him. She told everybody hello, managed to give each boy a little pat or a compliment. Making points, her specialty.

"I liked your column last week, Francis," she said. "Super!"

Flattered, the editor said, "I'm thinking about doing a column on you next week, Katie. What do you say?"

"On *me*?" Hand on bosom, nice girlish gesture. Phony, phony, Dana thought bitterly.

"Well, you were the first girl in the school's history to get a standing ovation at the cheerleader tryouts. But I'll need facts. Previous school; prior pep squad experience. And to whack it up a little, a few hard, investigative questions." He looked grim.

Katie clasped her hands behind her. "Give me a sample question."

"I've got one," Dana cut in. "Do you think it's demeaning to a girl to cater to jocks?"

"We don't 'cater' to them, Dana," said Katie, loftily. "You make us sound like cocktail waitresses. In the first place, we do most of our practicing in Pep Squad P. E., so—"

"Ah, but the cookie clause!" Dana said. "The camp fees. The cost of megaphone paint—"

Katie crossed her arms, defensive now. "I make cookies for my little brother anyway, so it's no big sacrifice to bake a few more for the players."

"What's the total cost of being a cheerleader?" Francis asked, scribbling in a notebook.

"Oh, I don't know—three hundred dollars—"

Dana hooted. "You pay that kind of money just to yell and jump up and down?"

"Well, there are uniforms, pompons, pep camp —it's an *activity*, like a sport, or acting. We wouldn't do it if we didn't like it. I guess it all depends on your point of view. Hey, can I change the subject?" she asked. "I need a bird."

There was instant silence. People looked at Dana, who blinked, then tightened up in suspicion. "What for?" he asked.

"Actually, it's a secret. Will you sell me one? A little bird that doesn't cost too much?"

Though he knew they were all watching him, Dana was numb and helpless under the wattage of her innocent blue eyes. He began to hyperventilate. His ears buzzed. Katie interested in birds?

"Well, sure," he said. "The cheapest is a normal peachface, a very pretty green bird with a red face and blue tailfeathers. I wholesale them for thirteen, but to girls with hickies on their necks the price is five, plus a bag of cookies."

Katie touched the blemish on her throat, actually blushing.

"Hey, fantastic!" she cried, patting his arm.

School bells were ringing, and bells were ringing in Dana's head. Impulsively, he grabbed her hand and squeezed it. He had a terrible, wonderful feeling that life would never be the same. The bars were down between them. Love could start, now.

"Do you want it for a pet?" he asked. "I've got a couple of hand-fed birds—"

She put her finger to her lips. "For a biology project, actually. I'm going to do a study of birds," she whispered.

"No kidding! Well, what if—"

But she was gone.

He plodded after her like a lovestruck farm boy.

7

Mr. Lockwood called the class to order. He was a bull-necked man with perhaps the last butch haircut in the West. He wore a tan suit with a brown shirt and a solid brown tie, and looked like a leftover Fascist. The shuffling of feet and papers subsided as he printed some words on the tan chalkboard. He turned, wiping chalk dust from his hands.

"Students intending to take biology next year will be required to submit an outline for a project this year," he said. "Sorry, no credit. But it will work toward your grade next year. Hands on how many are planning to take Biology II?"

Dana raised his hand. All he wanted out of the course was genetics, but to get the hamburger, he had to buy the wrapper, too.

"—Quinn, Cummings, Furlong—is that a hand, or a scratch, Norman? A hand. Norman, Rosillo. Quinn?—Electronics, I presume?"

Dana noticed a sneaky twinkle in his eyes.

Lockwood was a blindside tackler. What was he up to now?

"Yes, sir," said Paul. "The approach—"

Lunkhead struck. "Electronics, Quinn, is not part of the science of biology. Should think you'd know that. You'll have to come up with something else. Norman?"

Dana was embarrassed for his friend. But Paul must have thought of that, of course, so perhaps the show wasn't over.

"Uh, sir—" Paul removed his glasses and held them up to see whether they were dirty. "Didn't you tell us that biology is the science of living organisms and vital processes, et cetera?"

"Roughly." Mr. Lockwood spread his feet, getting into his debating stance.

"Then electronics can be part of biology when it affects an organ such as the human auditory nerve, *nicht wahr?*"

Everyone was listening. Contests between Paul Quinn and Mr. Lockwood were always worth trying to follow.

Lockwood scowled, his computer flashing warnings. *Cannot process this. Information garbled. Clarify.*

"Nonsense. If it doesn't have any bearing on the *action* of the auditory nerve—" He hesitated. He hated new ground.

"It does have," Paul said earnestly. "You see, it's an application of audio electronics that *by-*

passes the eardrum in order to avoid interference patterns, not to mention diffraction caused by objects in a room where the subject—"

"Still sounds like electronics to me," said Mr. Lockwood. "Furlong—"

Paul crossed his arms and raised his voice a few decibels, his manner expressing a laudable wish to be patient with someone a little retarded.

"Mr. Lockwood, it's the *application* of it—the way it stimulates the human hearing apparatus—that my project will deal with. I intend to create a more accurate sound pattern by doing away with loudspeakers—"

"Hope you're not talking about headphones?" Lunkhead hooted.

Kids laughed.

"Definitely not. It will employ tiny transducer/receptors pressed behind the ears, stimulating the aural nerves *directly* and taking a shorter pathway to the brain's sound-receptor centers. In other words—substitute ears!"

A boy pretended to rip his ears off.

"Put it in writing so I can see what you're trying to say," Lockwood said gruffly, then swerved his small eyes to Dana's face.

"Furlong, I hope it isn't birds again. If I hear one more chirp in this classroom—"

"It's birds," Dana said bleakly. "I'm going to prove that owls can be used instead of poisons in rodent control."

"Oh, my gawd," Lunkhead groaned. "You're serious, aren't you? Hardhats, everybody! Here come the owls!"

Kids pretended to duck marauding owls as Lunkhead urged them on, hands on hips, leering, Mussolini on the podium.

"Project Owl," Dana continued, doggedly, "was suggested by an experiment in Morristown, New Jersey. Poisons weren't working, and somebody who knew about owls suggested trying them against the rats and mice."

"An owl a day keeps a mouse away?"

"Would you believe *thirty-five* mice? A barn owl will eat dozens of mice a day. I've already persuaded a lot of people in my neighborhood not to put out poisons, because if an owl eats a poisoned mouse, it will die, too."

"Furlong, old fellow," the teacher said patronizingly. "Owls travel a long way on their little wings. How long do you think this owl will stay around once you open the cage?"

Dana smiled, waiting for the laughter to die. "I've already got two owls working for me. A scientist at my dad's plant gave them to me as nestlings. I keep them in a box on an old water tower near our house. I've even let them out at night. Now I'm leaving dead lab rats in their box to encourage them to nest there. It worked in Morristown."

Lockwood beamed. "Morristown, the off-Broadway of birdland. But if you'll promise to keep them out of my wife's hair, Furlong, I'll approve the project. —Norman, my dear, I'm sure it's not birds with you!"

Katie turned pink, covered her mouth, and giggled. Her blush deepened the birthmark on her cheek, which had the magical effect of making her even more beautiful in Dana's eyes.

"I'm sorry!" she said. "It *is* birds!"

Lunkhead staggered to his chair and sat down. "Birds," he said.

"I—um, want to compare the by-products of stress in human beings with stress in birds."

"Birds," Lunkhead said again. "Go on, dear."

"I'll make blood tests on birds under stress. I'll check for lactates and other by-products of stress, such as—"

Lockwood began to look interested. "How will you stress them?"

"With electric shocks, cages too low to perch in, and bright lights."

There was a ripple of movement, a rustle of whispering. Katie shocking a bird out of its wits? Jailing it? Blinding it? Dana sat up, not sure he had heard what he thought he had.

"No—seriously," he said. "What's the project?"

Katie sounded hurt. "Seriously, Dana, it *is* my project."

"But what's the point?" he blurted.

"The point—" she swallowed, "is that animals

get so cruelly mistreated in pet shops. I want to study what happens to them, with the idea of using the information in legislation—"

"I'm not hearing this," Dana said. "Legislation?"

"I would say she has a very valid point," Mr. Lockwood said happily. "It's true that animals do get mistreated in pet shops, although I think the Humane Society exaggerates—"

Katie gave him a grateful smile. "I thought it might help in diagnosing problems like feather-plucking, too—"

The class found the term funny. A plague of feather-plucking swept the room.

"What do you know about birds?" Dana asked coldly. He was not sure whether she was bugging him, or simply had a cruel streak in her that she thought was perfectly normal.

"Not much, yet," said Katie, "but before I'm through—"

"Any reason you couldn't study guinea pigs? They carry them in pet shops, too."

"But there's been so much work done on guinea pigs, and almost none on birds."

"There's no sense in it, woman! I can tell you all you need to know about stress in birds, and you don't need to torture one. It—it's cruel."

Katie looked at Mr. Lockwood, then sighed. She said quietly, "I don't see that it's any more cruel than torturing guinea pigs, Dana."

"But it's not *necessary!* Physiologically, guinea pigs resemble people, so that stressing them makes sense. But it isn't necessary to stress a bird. They don't share diseases with people," he lied.

"People get parrot fever," Katie murmured.

Lunkhead laughed loudly and pointed at Dana. "Too-shay, Furlong! Well, it's oh-eight-hundred hours, and time to get your pickled mice—"

"Actually," Dana said, as the students began to migrate to the lab tables around the walls of the room, "it isn't oh-eight-hundred *hours,* it's just oh-eight-hundred."

"Oh, thanks, Furlong. Gee, you're bright," Lockwood sneered.

Dana took a purple marking pen from the pocket of his notebook and uncapped it. As he passed Katie, he slashed a large X across the back of her hand. She looked at him, hurt.

"Why?" she wailed.

"Dwid of the Week Award," he said. "Take my advice, Senator, and stay out of bird torture. Or the ASPCA will be putting piranhas in your orange juice. To study the death convulsions of cheerleaders."

8

Katie, fumbling with her notebook, gazed at the crooked X Dana had slashed on her hand. Why did I do it? she thought dismally. I'm not going to do a study of lovebirds. Why did I say I was? I wanted to get his attention; but I didn't have to make a fool of him in front of his friends. Now I've really done it.

The classroom noises faded as Amanda Allen—English, second period—gazed out over the room, counting heads. She was tall and slender, and wore her dark hair long. Katie was surprised to notice a sort of halo effect, a soap-bubble shimmer, around her! How odd! Now she was speaking, but Katie had to strain to catch her words, which had the broken quality of a defective tape recording.

"Annie? Wish you . . . mind? . . . very . . . Herrick . . . by Annie Markley . . . aloud?"

The girl beside Katie went to take a sheet of paper from Mrs. Allen's hand. Katie felt weak.

There was a chill in the room, and the noises were definitely fading like distant radio signals. She gazed around, and gasped. The room was floating in air! Like a space platform, or a magic carpet. And then she realized what was happening, and tried to rouse herself to prevent it.

Not now! she thought, panic-stricken. You can't leave now, not in the middle of . . .

But there they came, the unmistakable chill, the lightheadedness, and the hollow-boned sensation, that foretold a visit to her other planet. And suddenly the classroom was gone, and she was on a sunny beach, with gray sand around her, blue water beyond, and a lone palm tree. And voices—a boy's voice—Ruben Lara's.

"The guards just brought in a drowning case, Dana! It looks like Katie Norman!"

Hovering somehow, like a gull, she saw him and Dana run down to the wet sand. It was a cool morning, with few sunbathers around. A cluster of surfers surrounded the girl lying on the sand, where a guard in red trunks knelt taking her pulse. Dana went to his knees and started giving her mouth-to-mouth, but the guard said, "No use, fella. No heartbeat. There's the doctor now. . . ."

Dana rose slowly, looking dazed. Katie wore a one-piece blue swimsuit that revealed the tender beauty of her body. Her hair gleamed on the dark sand. From a beach house on a low cliff nearby there floated a sound of music. It was sad and beautiful.

The doctor jogged up, carrying a bag.

"Which brings us to Katie Norman," Mrs. Allen's voice said, from somewhere beyond the beach. "Will you read, Katie?"

Katie murmured in her sleep. The music was lovely and she was happy.

The doctor thrust a long hypodermic needle directly into her heart. A newspaper photographer knelt and snapped a picture.

"She was always so cheerful," Dana said. "It had to be accidental."

The guard frowned. "I wonder—she kept swimming out, and I lost track of her. Then—"

"Did she have any friends?" the doctor asked.

"Friends!" Ruben said. "She knew everybody."

The doctor rose. "I didn't ask that. I asked if she had any friends, people she could really talk to about her problems."

"I don't know," Dana confessed. "I hate to think I might have helped her, and didn't—"

The photographer took another picture. A man asked him if he could get a print. "She was really beautiful, wasn't she?"

Then Katie saw the gypsylike young woman standing on the sand. She beckoned to Dana and he, puzzled, went to her.

"Don't blame yourself," she said to him, with her sad smile. "If anyone's at fault, it's me. I'm her real mother. I deserted her when she needed me. Girls need their mothers. . . ."

"Mama—?" Katie said. But the woman could not hear her.

"Katie? Are you with us?"

A hand on her arm. The doctor? No. Darkness was falling over the scene, and, fearing darkness, she opened her eyes. She had trouble bringing things into focus. But like a wakened sleepwalker, she knew suddenly where she was. Mrs. Allen was standing in the aisle beside her, leaning down to peer into her face.

"Oh!" Katie said, weakly. "I guess I dozed off. I baby-sat last night, and—what did you ask me, Mrs. Allen?"

"Your poem, Katie," said the teacher. She peered into Katie's eyes as though she could see through them right into her brain. "You'd better tell your people to get home earlier on school nights, hadn't you?"

"Yes. Okay! I wrote—oh, here it is. Shall I read it?"

"Please do," said Mrs. Allen, returning to her desk. She sat down and waited.

"Okay, it's a takeoff on a poem by, uh, Thomas Edward Brown, 1830 to 1897, called 'My Garden.' "

Mrs. Allen smiled. "Bet I can recite it, Katie! I was so charmed by that little poem when I was your age that I memorized it. Let's see—'A garden is a lovely—' No." She pondered.

Katie smiled happily and waited. Amanda began again.

" 'A garden is a lovesome thing, God wot!
  Rose plot,
  Fringed pool,
Fern'd grot—
  The veriest school of peace; and yet the fool
Contends that God is not—
Not God! In gardens! when the eve is cool?
  Nay, but I have a sign;
  'Tis very sure God walks in mine.' "

The students applauded. Amanda beckoned to Katie. Carrying the notebook, Katie went forward.

"Ummm, okay. It's called, 'My Porsche.' By Katie Norman. 1966 to—date unknown.

"A Porsche is a fearsome thing, God wot!
  Leather buckets,
  Walnut dash,
Double pot,
  The veriest pool of power. And yet the fool
Contends that power's not—
Not power! In the cockpit! When the driver's cool?
  Nay, but I have a sign.
  'Tis very sure I'll die in mine.

". . . It's a sort of burlesque. Parody? I don't know." She hurried to her seat.

Amanda was looking at her, dumbfounded. The kids were quiet. When the silence grew uncomfortable, Katie added, "It's kind of the way race drivers feel, I think."

"How *do* they feel?" asked Annie Markley, who, in Katie's opinion, was a teenage version of Mrs. Allen, a philosopher-busybody.

"Like they love and fear the beast. Not many race drivers die old."

"Then why do they race?" Annie asked.

"*I* don't know! Ask them. Maybe it's a death wish. But I think it's probably just that they, you know, love speed, and they're kind of wild and crazy guys. —Well, gee, it's just a poem," she giggled.

There was some written work, and, as the hour ended, Mrs. Allen returned some papers On Katie's essay—"Hemingway's Last Year"—she had written A+, and, *Please see me after class.*

Oh, no, you don't, Katie thought. We're not going to discuss my blackout! No way!

But as she hurried toward the door, the teacher called, "Katie?"

Katie stopped and waited, her mouth sullen. Amanda dealt with a couple of other students who had lingered, shooed them out, and invited Katie to sit near her desk.

Katie took a seat, and Mrs. Allen gazed at her in curiosity. "Well!" she said, finally. "That was quite a poem, Katie. Interesting, but a letdown at the last."

Katie shrugged. "I don't know. I thought it was pretty good."

"Good enough for a C, at least."

"A C!"

"For lack of logic. What has suicide to do with power?"

Katie was relieved; apparently Amanda wasn't going to ask about her trance. She said glibly, "I didn't say suicide, Mrs. Allen. I said 'die.' "

"Dying on purpose is known as suicide. And what has that to do with power?"

Katie toyed with a pencil.

"I don't know. Isn't it a sort of power if you can quit, like Hemingway, when things get hopeless? He'd had electroshock and everything, and there was nothing left for him. That's all I meant."

"But we're talking about Katie Norman, not Ernest Hemingway," the teacher said, with a smile.

Katie sighed. "Mrs. Allen, it's just a *poem!* My gosh! It's not my philosophy of *life* or anything."

Amanda was peering right into her head again, "Sure about that?"

Katie turned to gaze at the chalkboard. She had an uneasy feeling that Amanda might have ESP or something.

"Yes, ma'am," she said. "I'm sure."

"Okay. So much for that. There's one other thing, and then you can go. I was a little disconcerted by your trance, or whatever it was."

Katie shrugged.

"I fell asleep. I told you—the people—And after—"

Amanda waited until Katie ran down. "Is there something troubling you?" she asked. "You're new at Santo Tomas, and a move to a new school is always difficult. If there's anything upsetting you, I'd like very much to help."

Katie shook her head. "No! There's no problem. Oh, I didn't exactly like transferring at midterm, but the kids are okay, and I guess my work is alright."

"It's fine. But woolgathering, and poems like that, concern me. Let me know if you decide anything's wrong, won't you? I'd like to help."

Katie gathered her books, squeezed off a smile, and said, " 'Kay, Mrs. Allen! But I wish you wouldn't worry about me. I'm fine."

9

"The acoustics in here," said Paul Quinn, "would make a bowling alley operator weep."

"Speak up," Dana said, his mouth full of Spanish rice. "I can't hear you. The acoustics—"

An incessant, chiming clatter of silverware assaulted the ears. Dishes were being dumped into trays, and voices rattled like ping-pong balls off the walls and ceiling of the students' cafeteria. Paul put his lips near Dana's ear, like a racetrack tipster.

"Annie said Katie came on kind of strange in Mrs. Allen's class," he said.

"She came on strange in biology, if you ask me. What did she do?"

"Fell asleep. Out like a light."

"Best thing, maybe," Dana said jeeringly. But he was miserable over the way things had fallen apart for him and the cheerleader. It was all over. She could get stuffed. She wouldn't make a fool of him again.

A boy came up to talk to Paul, and Dana concentrated on his Spanish rice. Maybe she had been teasing him about torturing a bird. But why? Because, basically, he decided, she didn't like him. She liked athletes. She liked big muscles and thick necks.

"How much have you got to spend?" Paul asked the boy. Dana listened, disinterested.

"About a hundred and sixty dollars," the boy said. "I shoveled manure at a stable all last summer and managed to save that much. I've got a receiver-amp, but I must need new speakers. The sound is kinda woolly."

"You should have saved the manure," Paul said. "That's about all you can buy in state-of-the-art audio for a hundred and sixty." The boy looked crestfallen, and Paul laughed. "Well, actually, I don't think you need a load of tweeters and woofers anyway. Take about seventy dollars and buy a stereo frequency analyzer. It will intensify any range you want. Then give me the ninety you've got left and I'll buy myself some records."

Ruben Lara came up, leaning on the table beside Dana. "Going to Moonlight Beach Saturday?" he asked.

Dana roused from his glum reverie. "Maybe. Don't know."

"That beginner's board I told you I was finishing up? I need a guy to test it for me who isn't a dynamite surfer. No hard feelings," he said, with a smile, "but I thought you might be my man."

"Sure. I'll try out the board, if you'll come the bird consortium."

"Okay. If it looks right to you, it looks right to me."

Ruben left, and Dana gazed gloomily at Katie at the far end of the room, eating with some athletes. The hickie thing bothered him. He imagined her sitting in a parked car with some gasping Romeo last night, a guy with more arms than an octopus, more hands than a Hindu god.

Then he saw Francis Goodman appear in the aisle with a slip of paper in his hand, looking for someone. How did Dana know Francis was looking for him? He knew; everything today was weird, and here Francis was coming through the trestle tables to lay the paper beside his plate!

"Mrs. Allen asked me to bring you this," he said. "It's marked *Urgent*."

Dana unfolded the paper, as Francis moved away.

"Everything Amanda sends is marked *Urgent*," Dana said. "The only other category is *Emergency*."

Still, it was intriguing to read the note and learn that she wanted to see him in her room immediately after school, on *Urgent and Confidential* business. He'd been to her home with other kids occasionally, for soft drinks, popcorn, and discussion of something she wanted to see set in motion at school. And once it was an invitation to them to fly to London that Easter vacation with her and her husband.

Something to take his mind off Katie Norman, at least. He burped. Either he had developed a stomach ulcer, or Katie had done some damage in the area of his heart. He hurt.

Amanda was grading papers in her room when he slouched in. Pencils were stuck in her hair like feathers in an Indian brave's. She looked up with a big smile when she saw him.

"Hi! Close the door, will you? And sit here."

Dana took a seat in the front row. He learned immediately that whatever else the interview achieved, it would not take his mind off Katie.

"What's your opinion of Katie Norman?" Amanda asked, apparently completely serious.

Dana slipped into a modified horizontal position in the chair. "Katie who? Don't believe I know her."

"Oh, Dana," Amanda said, and laughed. "Santo Tomas is a small world. I've known ever since she hit the campus that you were infatuated with her. It was love at first sight, wasn't it? Don't kid me, boy. I see you walking to classes with her. Once I saw you buy her an apple from the apple machine. Some tribes regard that as the equivalent of a proposal of marriage. The Apple Machine Rite. But since about ten o'clock this morning, I've known that something's gone wrong between you."

She was teasing, but he suspected that it was done with serious purpose. "News to me," he said.

Amanda held a pencil between the tips of her index fingers, as though completing an electrical circuit. "Mr. Lockwood is not my favorite colleague," she said, "but in the teachers' lounge this morning he was telling us about Katie's embarrassing you in a debate over the torture of birds. At least according to him."

"Oh, that," Dana said. "Okay, what the heck, we had a little discussion."

"Which has left you pretty mad," Amanda Allen said. "But don't worry. She was just making sure you knew she was there."

Dana yawned. "Uh-huh. Is that all, Amanda?"

"Not quite. I'm sure it's hard for you to believe that it was actually a sort of pass on her part," the teacher went on, "but it's true. She likes you, Dana. Annie Markley tells me she mentions you often."

Dana was hungry to hear more, but loath to reveal his need. So he shrugged again, while the teacher smiled at him.

"Her approach, Annie says, is to joke about how steady you are, how stable. About your calculator being your rosary."

Dana grinned wryly. "And that proves she likes me?"

"It doesn't matter what she *says,* Dana, it's the fact that she mentions you all the time. You're on her mind, which makes you the very man I need to help on a project of great importance."

Dana's curiosity shot up like a fever. He yearned to believe she was right; but all the arrows seemed, to him, to point in the opposite direction. "It does?" he said.

The teacher smiled. "Trust me, Dana. As I'll have to trust you not to repeat anything I say from this point on."

He deliberated a moment. "Sure, Mrs. Allen. Scout's honor."

Amanda came and took a seat beside him. "I'm involved in a crash study of what goes on behind Katie's facade, Dana. But it's like deciphering the enemy's code. She's got problems, but she refuses to talk to me about them. Then today, I had a great idea: I'd get you to pick her lock!"

"Why would she talk to me?"

"Maybe she won't, but she's *dying* to talk to somebody. Authority figures like me, and the school counselor, are out. She distrusts us. I've tried to talk to her mother and father, too, but there's nothing cooking there, either. Twice I've asked her mother to come to school for a conference, but she writes back on company stationery that she's too busy. Her father is in and out of the country like a smuggler, so I haven't been able to catch him. Now I'm down to my final option: getting you to do my detective work for me."

She smiled and patted his hand.

Dana was pleased but embarrassed. "Okay. I'll get a magnifying glass and a Sherlock Holmes hat."

"Or how about, for openers, asking her for a date?"

Dana struck his brow. "You should have been in biology this morning! Waste of time. But, what the heck, I'll think about it." He started to gather his books. He knew now that Amanda's plan was hopeless. But he'd ask Katie anyway, sometime.

Amanda shook her head. "No time for thinking, Dana," she said crisply. "Katie's on a collision course with something very serious. I found that out yesterday, when I called the school she transferred from and asked whether she had any record of emotional disturbance there."

Dana hesitated. Disturbance? Katie? "Are we talking about the same cheerleader?" he asked. "Small, blond, peppy—?"

". . . and seriously disturbed. That's the one," the teacher said. "I found out that she had no record—unless I included a couple of small accidents she'd had."

She paused, holding him like a wrestler with her gaze. He waited for her to continue, and when she did not, he asked, feeling like a ventriloquist's dummy, "What kind of accidents, Mrs. Allen?"

"Automobile, Dana. One-car—ran right off the road twice, while she was still on her learner's permit. Tell me about one-car accidents," she suggested. "What do you know about them?"

He had read about one-car accidents somewhere, a rather startling statistic. A trickle of anxiety voltage ran through him. "Well, hmm," he said, shifting uncomfortable. "I'm not sure. . . ."

"Don't be afraid of the word," Mrs. Allen told him. "Refusal to recognize the problem is the reason it happens so often."

He said, "I think I've read that one-car accidents are a sort of—well—suicide threat. But—with Katie—nah, you don't know her."

"Oh?" Amanda Allen said. "Dana, I've counseled a lot of suicidal kids, and believe me, they don't all pace up and down waving suicide notes and carrying bottles with a skull-and-crossbones on them. Suicide is the number one cause of death among teenagers, even peppy ones. And yet nearly all suicidal kids are begging to be talked out of it. They're scared and hopeless. They leave clues lying around telling us that they've got problems, hoping somebody will intervene. I've tried, and usually succeeded, when I've come across their clues."

Dana tried to get his head working again, but it seemed to be on Hold.

"Katie kill herself?" he said. "Why would she?"

"I don't know, Dana. Let's try to find out, shall we?"

"Well—I mean, has she left any clues?"

Amanda reached for a looseleaf page lying on her desk and handed it to him without smiling. A poem was written on it. Dana immediately recognized Katie's neat, cursive style of printing. He read the poem, frowned, read it again, then looked up, puzzled.

"Well, it's—black humor, I suppose," he muttered.

"Think so? I don't."

"I mean, it's like saying, 'If I flunk that test, I'll cut my throat.' Isn't it?"

"No, Dana, it's like saying, 'Please, don't *let* me cut my throat!' It's part of a pattern. There were the automobile accidents. There was the day she couldn't get her eyes open after a reverie in Mrs. Martin's French class, and had to be led to the nurse! An aspirin or two and she was fine. But she'd made a statement, right? Drawn attention to unhappy Katie Norman. Then there was her falling asleep in my class this morning. And there are her book reports on famous suicides. Statements, clues, pleas! It's classic, Dana! Katie is thinking very seriously of taking her life."

Dana reread the last line of the poem. " *'Tis very sure I'll die in mine*." But none of what Mrs.

Allen had said fitted into the personality of the teasing girl he knew, who attracted him to her and then drove him away.

But two automobile accidents in a few months? That's not just fooling around, man, he told himself.

"Then shouldn't she be talking to a shrink?" he asked.

"Of course. But she won't even admit there's a problem. So what's my next move? You're the only one I can think of."

For some reason, Dana turned the page over, as if there might be one of Amanda's "clues" on the back of it. There was—at least there was something. There were the initials, *D.F.*, in a very flowery box, and another version of the little caricature of him she had done on his lab write-up.

He *was* on her mind. At least that much was true.

Mrs. Allen took the paper from his hand, looked at it, and returned the page to her desk. "I hadn't seen that myself. What do you say, Dana?"

"I don't know where to start," he murmured. "Ask her for a date? To what?"

"Don't you and your friends go to Moonlight Beach on Saturdays?"

"Usually." He felt a familiar weight of incompetency descending on him. He was a lot better with birds than he was with people. He couldn't "sell." Was a weak-kneed debater. Couldn't fake enthusiasm he didn't feel. He was, in short, the clod Katie hinted he was.

"Invite her along!" the teacher urged. "A couple of hours on the sand, listening to the waves and soaking up sunshine and uncomplicated affection—I forgot to ask whether you really do like her. That's an important part of it."

"Sure. She's—I really like her." He tried a grin.

Amanda smiled. "Katie knows, of course, and that's one reason she's picked you; the other being that she feels the same way about you. So how about letting her know how you feel? Little by little it will come out—the truth about Katie Norman."

Dana stood up, collected his books, looked out the window. "I suppose I could telephone her tonight—"

"You don't need to. She's got cheerleader practice right now. Go on down and talk to her during a break. Tell her you're sorry about the purple X on her hand—and see where it leads."

10

Down at the edge of an outdoor basketball court, some boys were cheering the pep squad girls. "Shake it, shake it!" a boy yelled, as the girls did a jump. Dana stood on the sidelines with his tote bag at his feet.

"Alright, new girls, this is a spirit stick," cried the varsity girl who was leading the practice. Her voice was high and piercing. "When I raise it, scream. When I lower it, stop."

Dana located Katie in the group of girls in white sweaters and blue-and-white pleated skirts. He thought he could hear her voice as they screamed, then broke off, raggedly, as the leader swept the spirit stick down. All the girls were holding pompons, which they shook as they screamed.

The leader lectured them some more, then looked into a booklet. "Everybody got 'Hey, All You Mustang Fans' memorized? Alright, let's run through it, and end with a double hurkie."

After the yell, the senior girl said, "Take five,"

and sat down on the cement to study the booklet. The girls melted away to the sidelines or coalesced into blue and white droplets. Katie joined three other girls, her back to Dana.

He braced himself, and called, "Hey, Katie!"

She looked around, smiling, but went blank-faced when she saw him. He tried to keep himself inflated with confidence.

"You really got the moves!" he said.

She shrugged. He probably would have left right then, but remembering his promise to Amanda, he walked out to join her, self-conscious and grinning. She turned to face him, then dropped one pompon and began to crinkle the other with both hands. He saw, unfaded since this morning, her Dwid of the Week Award on the back of her hand.

"Hey, I'm sorry about that—" he said, grimacing at the purple X.

Katie sighed. "Marcia will love it."

"Put some powder base on it!" Dana suggested. "Like on your hickie."

At that her lips relaxed a little, and she touched her throat. "Maybe I'd better, Kapitan."

"Marcia's your sister?"

"Stepmother."

"Not the one in the car this morning?"

"Yep," she said. "Only nine years older than me. How about that?" She smiled.

Dana did not know what to say, but knew he

must keep talking. "I was just going to say, I'm sorry about the way I came on this morning. I guess it's no worse to torture a bird than it is a guinea pig. But I'm the Birdman of Encinitas, not the Guinea Pigman."

Another trace of a smile. Dana saw the leader get up and begin to switch her spirit stick around. He felt time leaking away.

"What I was thinking—you could study birds under conditions of normal stress," he blurted. "I'd be glad to take you to some wholesale bird farms, where the birds are kept in crowded aviaries. Would that help?"

"Might." Another measured smile. But a hint of satisfaction in her face, a little catlike stretching of certain muscles in her body as she moved.

"Do you surf, Katie?" Dana asked.

She frowned, smiled, giggled. "I don't know, I never tried."

"Well, listen, it's easy with a boogie board. My sister's got one, and . . . hey, some of us are going over to Moonlight this Saturday. Could you come along?"

The squad leader was calling for attention, and Dana wanted to yell at her to shut up, to let things happen. . . .

"You're *inviting* me? Surprise!" Katie said. "I shouldn't. I'm not even sure I could go, but—"

As the leader piped energetically, Katie began

to back away, smiling. She picked up her other pompon.

Hey, all you Mustang fans!

Stand up and clap your hands!

"You will?" Dana yelled.

"Yes!" Katie cried back.

"Thank you—I mean, I'll confirm later this week! We'll bring all the food, and I'll have my sister's boogie board, and I really do love you Katie, and don't worry, Amanda can help if there's a problem, and—"

Most of it was just in his head, where joyful noises were going on, and a kind of electricity was creating blue power in his veins. He slung his bookbag over his shoulder.

Now that you've got that beat,

This time let's stomp our feet!

He was sure he heard Katie's voice, and he looked back as he walked off, saw her look at him and shake a pompon in his direction.

He would call Paul as soon as he got home. About the bird deal, ostensibly, but it wouldn't be long before he was telling him about Katie, at least as much as his promise allowed him to.

11

Squinting at the dial, Katie set the microwave oven and put the hamburgers inside. The children she was baby-sitting tonight were setting the table.

"This boy at school said something bad to me," Dustin said. He was six, red-haired, and freckled, reminding Katie of a small ceramic effigy of an Irishman. If she watered his head, grass would spring up. "So I socked him."

"That's the stuff. Pour the milk, huh, Jill?"

In her mind there was the same dread she had felt the first time she drove the car off the road. *Dana, what are you up to?* she kept thinking, while the worry machine in her mind ran brokenly on, lurching over the debris of her fears. Why in the world had he invited her to the beach party, after the way she'd tormented him that morning?

Just before she left the house tonight, she'd thought she had it figured out.

He was going to stand her up! Let her spend an

hour on her hair, sneak a lipstick into her purse, get into her beach clothes—and then not show up.

But the idea shriveled. Because he wasn't like that. She might do it to him, but he wouldn't do it to her. He lived by a code as strict as the rules of backgammon.

Back to square one, when he'd left her at cheerleading practice. She was puzzled that he should have changed his mind about her so suddenly. It was a tremendous change in the ways of the slow-moving Science Major, with his glacierlike speed in courtship. What had shifted his gears for him? Why had he come plunging down to find her?

Another possibility, much worse, occurred to her.

He wanted to stop the guerrilla war with her and become a team. Just an average Santo Tomas couple, like Paul and Annie Markley or something. Then he could relax comfortably into the boy-girl thing, like tilting back in the television chair to watch a program. Sip a little Coke, pat his stomach. Good old steady Katie. Guess I'll call her after a while and see what's she's doing.

Well, I'll tell you what she's doing, buster! She's going bananas, and you aren't helping much!

Did you know her real mother dumped her when she was nine? She even tried to put her up for adoption once, while her father was out of the country. So she must have been a pretty screwy kid. Or was she? Dana, I'll be damned if I know! You tell me. I'd like to tell you some other things, too, but you'd panic. First you've got to get to know me. Wake up and look at me! Over here! The one with her eyes closed while she's driving seventy miles an hour!

Oh, sure, Dana, we'll just go steady for a while, and then some night when you're trying to put a hickie on my neck, I'll say, "Excuse me, Dana, but I tried to kill myself with sleeping pills the other night. Only I threw up. What would you suggest that I do about it?"

You'd be so shocked you wouldn't stop running till you reached the counselor's office and helped her get the net out of the closet.

"Katie?"

One of the kids was talking to her.

"Hmm?" Her mouth was full of hamburger, and she was moving her jaws, so they must have started dinner. Jill was peering at her across the table.

"I said, hurry up and eat so I can show you a valdez," Jill said.

Valdez? So there must have been some discussion of gymnastics. "Alright," she said. "And then I'll lead a cheer for you."

The kids bounced up and down in excitement, and Katie smiled.

After dinner they went to the living room. Katie took her stance for a yell. She had brought her new pompons, which needed to be broken in some more. She led a yell, then executed a double hurkie. Jill did a valdez—almost—and Dustin performed somersaults until Katie had to intervene to save the coffee table.

And at last they were in bed. It was eight-ten, and Dana would certainly call early this time and try to wrap up the cherryhead deal. She tingled. She liked to see how he came on when he had troubles he couldn't rinse out of his life with a little problem-solving shampoo. She wished she could bring up the subject of girls and ask what he thought about going steady. But he might catch on. She had to be careful; not make it too easy for him. They had to follow the scenario right up to the moment when he found her.

In the den, she installed herself at the desk, studied some French conjugations, and breezed through the vocabulary. When the telephone burred, she gave a start. She was ready with her patter, Trinidadian *patois* this time. Picking up the handset, she nestled the plastic against her ear.

" 'Allo?" she said.

At once she heard the voice of the Science Major, trying to keep his cool but betraying anxiety by speaking faster than normally. "Are you the party who advertised cherryhead lovebirds for sale?"

"Yes, mahn."

A pause. "Um . . . are they sold?"

"No, sah. Dey still out dere in de flight cage."

She heard Dana mutter something, then ask, "They're still for sale, then?"

"Well, yes and no, mahn."

"What does that mean? Are they for sale, or aren't they? Are they sick or something?"

"No, dey all be fine lookin' birds. Full of viga', excep' for one of de hens. I t'ink she got de French moult."

"That doesn't seem very likely, with peach-faces. How big an aviary are they in?"

"Plenty big. Six meter by two meter by three."

"I don't follow. The others are alright, but you won't sell *any* because one hen is moulting?" Dana's voice was rising.

"Dat right, mahn. If I sell dem and de others get sick, somebody t'ink I t'ief dem."

"I see. How did you get the birds?" Dana asked. "Did you raise them?"

"I keep some birdies in Trinidad, but my uncle died here and I came to close out de estate. Uncle Dieu got plenty peachface birds."

Dana did not speak for some time, then said soberly, "Well, I'll tell you what I think you should do. —What's your name, by the way?"

"Dey calls me Belle. How you call?"

"Dana. The same guy that's called you three times now, gel. And I think maybe you should know that playing tricks with a telephone is a plenty big federal offense."

"Oh, mahn, I not want nothing like that! What I do wrong?"

"You advertise birds that don't exist. For whatever reason I can't imagine, gel. But I'm going to report it to the police if it happens again. You get out of the classifieds, understand? You're messing up my bird market."

"But I only advertise dis one time, speak de business wit de people! Straight business proposition. You 'gree?"

"No, I don't agree. In fact, I'd like to go on record as saying that I'm glad I'm not messed up with a fruitcake like you. You're having an effect on bird prices with these insane offers you're making, and it had better stop."

The line emptied, the dial tone buzzed like an angry wasp. She hung up. Smiling, she punched the buttons on the telephone as though it were a computer, reflecting. He was coming closer. One of these nights he would walk in, stare at her incredulously, and say, "Katie! What do you think you're doing?"

And they could start.

Breathless, Katie opened *The Bell Jar* and started a report for Mrs. Allen on Sylvia Plath's suicide in London. There was, for her, a mystery in it. How could anyone kill herself by putting her head in a gas oven? The question was academic, of no particular interest to her personally, because in this area gas ovens were almost unknown. They were all electric or microwave, and who wanted to roast her head even for a good reason like suicide?

That gave her an idea for the theme of the paper.

What method would Plath have used in Southern California? Pills? A one-car accident? Razor blade? She took a little cutting tool out of her purse and slipped the guard back and forth so that the single-edge blade came out repeatedly like a serpent's tooth. She made the tiniest of nicks just over a wrist vein, not quite drawing blood. Then she shivered and put it away.

Could she work into the essay the reason why (she had read this) most wrist-cutters did it in the bathtub? Not to avoid the mess, but because if they were good coagulators, the cuts often healed before they could bleed to death. But the water prevented coagulation. She would work it in somehow, see what kind of comment Amanda made on the back of the page!

12

On Friday, in the cafeteria, Dana was eating with some friends when Katie stopped behind him. "Hi!" she said. "Are we still on for tomorrow?"

"You betcha."

"Well—here's how you get to *Chez Norman*." She laid at his place a three-by-five file card on which she had drawn a map, with her address neatly inscribed. She had used a tiny heart instead of a dot over the *i* in Hidden Valley Road. She had rubber-stamped her telephone number, and drawn little flowers in the corners.

"It's way out there," she said. "Sure you want to go through with this madness?" The boys smiled at her.

"Positive," Dana said. He studied the map. "That's out near Mockingbird Farms, isn't it?"

"Turn right at Mockingbird. Then follow the map. The natives are harmless, but don't give them any money. It encourages them to beg. And don't feed the yard crocodiles."

Dana smiled. "I know the area. I go by it on the way to San Marcos when I sell birds. I'd like to swing by a bird farm on the way to the beach. Okay? I'm selling a few."

"Super. I'd love to see the birds."

On Saturday morning Dana made the twenty-minute drive to the Mockingbird Farms area, a rustic subdivision that had never gotten beyond looking disheveled, and turned south on a winding two-lane strip of tar through lumpy hills covered with brush, eucalyptus, and oak groves. Only a few dozen homes had been erected in these almost virgin chaparral foothills. The cool air was redolent of sage, sweet and medicinal. He passed a horse farm with white fences, turned right on an even narrower road through lemon and live-oak groves, and popped up onto a ridge to see a large house with a red tile roof and not much of a yard.

A little boy was standing by the mailbox, which had NORMAN painted on it and some more of Katie's flowers. The boy waved at Dana as the Furlong Chevy slowed. Dana saw that he wore glasses. He had long hair as fine and soft as mink fur.

Dana got out. "Hi! Does Katie Norman live here?"

The little boy took his hand. He was about six. "Uh-huh. She said to bring you in. Daddy's home, too."

"What's your name?"

"Cunningham Norman. Katie calls me Cutepig. She's my *half*-sister."

Cunningham led him down some railroad tie steps toward the house. "Do you have a whole sister, too, or maybe another half?" Dana asked.

The little boy looked up at him through his spectacles as though he could not make him out very well. "No. Just Katie. Daddy's working, but he said he wants to meet you."

Cutepig opened the door, and a man called, "Hi! Come on in. Katie'll be right here."

From another room Katie's voice trilled, "You're five minutes early, Kapitan!"

"Sorry!"

Dana and his guide, who reminded him of a small, lovable pet, were gazing into a large living room, like the *sala* of a Mexican ranch house. He was intrigued by a bath towel spread on the floor under his feet, and sniffed spray disinfectant in the air. Through an expanse of plate glass he could see a young and tender lawn with bald spots, heaps of bricks and earth, and strings pulled taut between stakes. Cunningham led him into the *sala*, where a man of about forty lounged on a long leather sofa, wearing old slacks and sandals, a t-shirt, and holding a clipboard. Sipping from a can of beer, he offered his hand to Dana, smiling.

"I'm Katie's father," he said. "Sit down. Furlong, is it? Eight Furlongs equal a mile, eh? Guess I can't offer you a beer. Child labor law or something."

Dana gazed around. "Just moved in?"

"Not long ago. And we may be moving out again before long. Tough life. Business like crop-picking."

Dana sat near him, with Cunningham on his right. The little boy continued to cling tightly to his hand as though he were drowning. Dana could not retrieve it without actually yanking it free.

"What kind of business are you in?" he asked.

"Education—projects for the State Department. Sometimes it means a two-year tour of duty out of the country. Looks like another one coming up."

Dana felt a pang of disappointment. Katie leaving! Then a moist sensation inside his right elbow startled him, reminding him of childhood episodes of bed-wetting. When he looked down, Cunningham was licking his arm! He muttered and pulled his arm free. Mr. Norman swore.

"Is he doing that again? Cunningham, Jesus Christ! You said when I gave you the Hot Wheels you'd cut that out."

"It's alright," Dana assured him, and patted the boy's head. Cunningham made choking sounds, then ran into the back of the house. Soon Dana heard him wailing.

"Hey, I'm sorry," Dana said. "It was alright—he just surprised me."

Mr. Norman sighed. "No, it isn't alright, dammit. His mother ought to quit working, so he'd see her once in a while. I'll go settle him down." He got up.

Dana wiped his arm with his handkerchief. A moment later a creature he hardly recognized came into the room. It was a naked blond girl—no, she was wearing the world's scantiest bikini. She was pulling on a tan blouse, and looked absolutely spectacular, much sexier than the girlie magazine chicks, who looked, most of them, like dairy animals. She pulled on green slacks.

"What's the matter with Cutepig?" she asked. "Hi, Kapitan."

"Same old thing," said her father, as he started out. "Listen, have fun, kitten. Bring her home in one piece, Dana."

"No fear, Mr. Norman. I'm majoring in Driver's Ed. Tell Cutepig we'll bring him back a starfish and—and some candy."

"That'd be nice. He gets lonesome. If we stay in California, we'll have to move closer in."

"That's an idea," Katie said with enthusiasm. "I'm getting tired of long lonely walks through lemon groves, like the ghost of Sylvia Plath."

Dana looked at her. Sylvia Plath! Hadn't the writer killed herself? Was Katie doing a report on her, now? My God.

They went out. As Dana started the car, Katie sighed.

"I'm sorry about Cutepig. So *embarrassing!* He keeps doing that. Practically every week Marcia has a session with his Montessori teacher, trying to cure him of licking people."

But Amanda Allen can't get Marcia to Santo Tomas even once to talk about your problems!

"It did kind of surprise me," Dana admitted. "Maybe—" He hesitated, as they headed down through the hilly lemon groves.

"Maybe what?"

"Maybe he'd do better if you didn't call him Cutepig. It's such a pet name. He kind of reminds me of a pet boy. Maybe it makes him think of himself as a baby instead of a rapscallion."

"Well, he's hardly more than a baby," Katie retorted, "and I've brought him up practically by myself, and I *like* Cutepig."

Dana laughed. "Oaky, okay! I just thought, like maybe he needs more kids to play with. What your father said."

Katie struggled to fasten her seat belts, and Dana helped her. The sweet fragrance of shampoo excited him.

"He needs friends," Katie agreed. "But Marcia thinks it's so healthy out here—"

"She means healthful," Dana said. He knew right away he shouldn't have, because it was like one of their old sniping routines, and he really had not meant to correct her. He was just making self-conscious conversation, and not very well.

Katie said wearily, "Oh, Lord, Kapitan, I might never have learned that if you hadn't told me. Thanks a million."

Dana grimaced. "Sorry. All I meant—"

"Was to put me down."

"No! Amanda Allen calls it footnoting. I've got to stop. Disgusting habit. Wish I'd never started."

Katie glanced at him strangely. "What's Amanda got to say about it?"

"In class. It's a failing. I accept responsibility. I will quit."

They passed Mockingbird Farms. The air blowing through the car was scented with lemon blossoms and dust. Dana realized he was making rapid progress in the wrong direction, and decided to start over.

"Your father said you might be moving. Where to?"

"I don't know. Nowhere, I hope. We've been to so many places I'm beginning to speak broken English."

"Did your real mother die? It's kind of unusual for the father to get custody, in California."

Katie looked out the other window. They were on a dusty side road to the bird farm Dana had mentioned. "No, she didn't die," she said.

Then her head turned quickly and she looked into his eyes. "Why all the questions?" she asked.

Startled, Dana said, "I don't know. I'm just curious. 'All About Katie.' An essay I'm doing."

"You've got a lot to learn, buster," Katie said. Then, at his expression of perplexity, she laughed, a brittle sound like Christmas tree ornaments breaking.

"Hey, I'm sorry," she said. "Only I know why you're cross-questioning me, and I don't appreciate it."

"I'm not cross-questioning you, I just—"

"You just heard from Paul, who heard it from Annie, that I fell asleep in Mrs. Allen's class, and you thought that was kind of weird. So you got to wondering about me."

"For Pete's sake!" Dana said. "I'm interested in you. As a girl. And your father told me you might be moving, and I hope you're not, but anyway I'd like to know you better while you're here."

Katie looked down the road, then laughed. "Alright. Start over. My real mother moved out when I was nine or ten. Tuberculosis, I think. Mandatory hospitalization. Then Daddy married Marcia. And here we are. Who's got custody of you?"

He looked at her, saw she was smiling, and the anxiety ran out of him. He had been fearful he'd blown the whole investigation.

"I'm the sorry product of an unbroken home,"

he said. "Father, mother, sister, me. I raise birds, Wendy collects plastic horses, my parents play bridge. Dad is a biochemist, I guess. Whatever he is, I'm supposed to become one, too. Unfortunately."

Katie looked at him, as if really interested, her slightly slanted eyes richly blue. They were non-cheerleader eyes, this time, and he had the odd impression that what he had just said was of great interest to her.

"Like father, like son?" she asked.

"Funny, my mother said that the other day, when she was trying to convince me I'm going to be a scientist like my father. But there is no way I'm going to make it, Katie. I suppose I'll go to Stanford, like he did, but—"

"So whatcha gonna do?" Katie said, seeming fascinated.

"I don't know. I really do not know. All I know is birds. Sell them door to door, maybe."

"Hmm," Katie said, and giggled. "Maybe you're more interesting than you seem."

He threw her an indignant look and she began laughing again.

13

Dana swung off the side road into a ramshackle collection of buildings. The car bounced over the ruts. Under the blue sky, palms and pink-flowered oleanders bestowed an exotic aspect on the whitewashed sheds and aviaries. Beneath an immense eucalyptus tree was a small frame house. Katie was charmed by the tumbledown bird ranch.

"The poor man's Tahiti!" she said. "Is this the old Paul Gauguin place?"

"This is the old Bill St. John place," Dana said. "Big wholesaler. I'll make out like a bandit today. Got four fine black-masked lovebirds to sell, at forty per. Absolutely primo little birds."

He lifted the small carrying case of birds from the trunk, and they walked toward the salesroom. A scarlet macaw on a gabled stand in the yard squawked at them, and Dana lifted the huge bird onto his hand and made it kiss him with its great black beak. Katie backed off.

"Look out! He could bite your head off."

"Could, but wouldn't," Dana grinned. "Big difference."

They entered the salesroom, where nesting boxes, cages, medicines, and books on birds were displayed. In the center of the room sat a wine barrel made into a cage; vivid finches made buzzing noises as they darted around like tropical fish.

A big, thick-chested man who looked like a sunburned dirt farmer came in from the back. "Hello, Dana," he said. "Watcha got there, kid?"

"Four nice black-masks," Dana announced, proudly placing the carrier on the counter. The little birds were green and yellow, with black heads, scarlet bills, and white eye-rings.

"Got 'em coming out of my ears," Bill St. John sighed. "But let's give 'em a physical."

Dana and Katie trailed him into a smaller room with a seed-littered counter and battered holding cages, where birds large and small created an impressive chatter. St. John closed the door and placed the carrying case on the counter. Humming, he opened the gate and reached inside to trap a bird.

"How's your social life?" he asked.

"Improving," Dana said with a grin.

St. John's fingers were thick and horny, and looked as though they would scarcely bend. The bird he pulled out chattered and tried to bite, but he held it so that its wicked little beak was unable to puncture his flesh.

Still humming, he looked the bird over, taking longer than usual to do so, although Dana knew the bird's breast muscle was exceptionally full, its vent clean—the first things a wholesaler checked.

"This is Katie Norman," he said. "She might want to look your aviaries over some day for a paper she's doing for a class at school."

St. John studied Katie across his thick spectacles, and murmured, "Proud to meet you, Katie." Then he went back to examining the bird. He held it to his ear and listened to its breathing, a curious procedure for a buyer who knew the seller; it was practically an accusation of lung infection.

"The paper's going to be on stress, Mr. St. John," Katie said.

"Plenty of stress in this business," said St. John. "Oh my God. You wouldn't believe it. Well, let's see. Head could be a little blacker—"

"What do you mean, blacker?" Dana cried. "It's out of a wild-caught African pair, no brown Fischer blood at all. Black as coal."

"Just kidding," St. John said. "Nice birds, Dana. I'll take 'em." He reached for a checkbook.

Dana relaxed, and winked at Katie. "Those are outstanding birds, Bill. Can't I get you up a dollar?"

"Up? I'm paying thirteen-fifty, this week," said Bill St. John.

Dana smiled. "You old kidder," he said.

"Wish I *was* kidding. Oh, hell, I'll go fifteen, but I may regret it."

Dana leaned on the counter and stared at the man. He felt numb, from head to foot. "What's the joke, Bill?"

"No joke. I was paying forty last month, but somebody's been selling blacks for ten dollars, which means the market's dropping and I'm going to have to cut my pay prices, too."

Dana smote his brow, stunned and furious. "No way, Bill! I've talked to that moronic bird girl, and she doesn't have Bird One. All she's got is a bird brain. She's nuts! She just runs these ads—"

"Not what I've heard, Dana," said the wholesaler. "I know of two parties, who I can't name, who've bought birds from her. Ten dollars a smash. Plus, there are thirty-five hundred wild-caught black-masks in the quarantine station at Chula Vista, and when they hit the market, the price is going to drop."

"Oh—bull!" Dana said, angry and disgusted. "That old quarantine station story . . . But somehow these mysterious birds never seem to reach the market." He licked his lips. "That's the best you can do?"

"Sorry. Like it or lump it."

Dana looked at Katie, who, bending from the waist, was now talking to a yellow-crowned Amazon parrot. "I'll lump it," he said. "I'm not hurting that bad. I'll hold them till this idiot girl quits running her ads."

St. John returned the bird to the carrier. "Sorry."

Dana said, "Let's go," and walked out.

"What happened?" Katie asked, as they drove from St. John's little Tahiti, which looked less like Paradise than ever.

Dana's hands clamped on the steering wheel hard enough to crush it. "*Damn!* Those birds are *perfect!*" he said. "And I'll get a decent price for them, too."

"But why wouldn't he buy them?"

Dana assumed she had heard the conversation in the buying room, but he was willing to repeat it. "Some—person, some—fruitcake, is running ads in the classifieds. Birds for peanuts. Three in the last ten days. And they're phony!"

"My goodness," Katie said. "Is it the same person each time?"

"Has to be. Although—God, I don't know," Dana groaned. "She uses different accents, and stories. But whether it's one girl or ten, you can see what's happening to the bird market."

He was driving fast, and breathing hard, muttering to himself. They passed a small shopping plaza. There was another one ahead where he often sold birds to a pet shop for more money than St. John paid him; unfortunately, small shops could not absorb much of his production.

"But I don't see why anyone would do such a thing," Katie said.

"Why, why, why?" Dana groaned. "Maybe it's a plot."

"Russian?" Katie said.

"No. But suppose three or four persons decided to work together to wreck the bird market. A kitten-sellers' cartel, say. They could run ads for a few months, and you can see what would happen—is *happening,* in fact. I've got birds I paid a couple of hundred dollars for—rare mutations. And an albino peachface I've bred that's worth six hundred. So how can I sell birds for twelve or thirteen bucks?"

They turned into the parking lot of the shopping plaza.

"Maybe it's a lonely person who just wants to talk," Katie said.

"For ten dollars a conversation?"

He parked. In the window of the shop a boa constrictor, thick as a motorcycle tire, writhed almost imperceptibly. Dana got the carrier out again and Katie followed him into the shop. The proprietor finished counseling a young woman about her neurotic Siamese, and asked Dana what he could do for him.

"Hi. I'm Dana Furlong. I've sold you birds several times—"

"Right. What've you got?"

Dana showed him the birds.

"How much?"

"Thirty dollars. I usually sell them to Bill St. John, but he's only paying twenty-five this month."

"Well, let's look them over."

Dana showed Katie crossed fingers as the proprietor carried the birds into a glassed-in holding room. He checked the birds out and, one by one, placed them in a small aviary among a couple of dozen other black- and blue-masked lovebirds. He came back.

"Nice birds, Dana. Cash or check?"

"Check, please."

In the car, Katie laughed. "Wow! Dana, you lied!"

He looked at her angrily. "Do you know what he'll sell those birds for? Fifty-five or sixty."

"But you still lied. Bill St. John is only paying fifteen. You said—"

"Bill's an old pirate. He'll be paying thirty again as soon as he loses his excuse to cut prices, and needs birds. And I didn't hear him say anything about his cutting selling prices, Katie."

Katie smiled happily as they drove toward the beach. "No, that's true. But it's kind of surprising, at that. You telling a lie. I thought you were feather-perfect."

"Oh, no. I have a mole near my navel, too. I'll show it to you when we get to the beach."

14

"What a neat day!"

Katie craned her neck to look at the beach as they coasted to the dead end. The sun showered its warmth on the scene like golden pollen. The beach was a pocket-sized paradise—a few palms, cliffs at the north and south ends of the white sand, waves lazily rolling in. Still irked, Dana bumped the curb as he parked. A subdued roar of surf came up.

"Looks like the surf is still up," he said. "I've got to try out a board for Ruben."

Blithe and cheerful, Katie gazed over the tropical scene. "It's like a pointillist painting! Dots of color everywhere. No two swimsuits the same color. Just like a palette."

"What's a pointillist painting?" Dana asked.

"It was an Impressionist technique. The artist used little dots of paint instead of brush strokes. The eye blended them. You don't know much about art, do you?"

He looked at her. She frowned, then laughed. "I'm teasing. Sorry."

Well, I don't feel like being teased, he felt like grumbling. Carrying their gear, they passed the lunchstand and plodded through the deep sand. He heard a dove cooing in a lone palm. At the north end of the beach a small, high-sided fishing boat was working the kelp bed. Waves roared in and crumpled into lace. People were snapping frisbies along the wet sand; a baby in diapers toddled away from its parents, squealing and laughing.

"Hi!" Annie Markley waved to them from where some straw mats were spread on the sand. A dark and pretty girl, she was oiling her legs; the others raised their heads from where they lay, and waved. Dana spread their mats beside them, tossing a blanket nearby.

"Katie, do you know everybody?" he asked. "Annie, Betty, Francis, Paul?"

"I haven't met Betty. I've seen you on the campus," Katie said. "And someplace else, haven't I?"

"Hamburger Heaven," Betty said. "I work there after school. I'll have to be there today, too, at three, darn it." She was a small chubby girl with a cherubic face. Her full features made Dana think of a little stone angel in a cathedral, blowing on a horn.

"Uh-huh, I've taken my little brother there," Katie said.

"As a matter of interest," Francis said, "Betty

says they throw out hamburgers that aren't sold within twelve minutes. Dana and Paul would think of that as a half-life of six minutes."

"No, I'd think of it as a terrible waste," Paul said. "If they could be quick-frozen—shipped to Cambodia—"

"Then the Cambodians would get as fat as me," Betty said.

"Oil my back?" Katie said to Dana, handing him a plastic bottle. She stripped off her slacks and blouse. As she lay facedown on a mat, he uncapped the bottle. He looked the area over with relish. Smooth flesh, lightly toasted, finely pored. He saw Paul smiling as he watched him. When he squirted some lotion on Katie's spine, she squealed.

"No, Dana! Warm it in your palm, first, dummy. Haven't you ever oiled anybody?"

"Sorry. Failed to take into account the temperature differential," Dana said. "The fact is, a sun-warmed body—"

"Computerize it for me, Kapitan," Katie said.

He felt a slight edge of irritation, though he knew that according to Amanda's theory she was just being sure she had his attention. He oiled her with smooth passes of his palm, feeling a warm thrill. Legalized pawing. Soon he would lie beside her, and maybe there would be a little eye-courtship, and some fingertip touching.

Then with a pang he remembered his promise

to test the board for Ruben. There would be no more good combers until tomorrow so he was locked into the promise.

"Where's Ruben?" He capped the bottle.

"Surfing," Paul yawned. "The board's over there—the red one." He lay down.

Dana saw a short, thick board stuck nose-down in the sand. "Beautiful," he remarked. "You could go through a hurricane on that log."

Annie sat up. "Did you come in your Porsche—God wot?" she asked Katie.

Katie was silent; Dana saw her hands clench for an instant. *"God wot"*: a phrase from her suicide poem! Had Amanda confided in Annie, too, or was the girl working on intuition?

"Wasn't that funny?" Katie said, finally. "The poem was supposed to be a joke, but Amanda took it so big. I felt like a ninny, trying to explain it to her. Ever try to explain a joke?"

"The rest of it was so straight that it misled her," Annie said. "I was fooled, too. Who's the young woman who brings you to school?" she asked.

"Marcia," Katie said.

Apparently she intended it for her answer. But Betty asked, "Your sister?"

"Stepmother. Nine years older than me. I loan her my *Seventeen* magazine and she loans me *Elle*."

The girls laughed. "Really? Only nine years?"

"Mm-hmm," Katie said.

"Bring her along sometime," Annie said. "I'll find a date for her."

"She's married to Katie's father, Annie," Betty said. "Don't be gross. She's pretty, though. What's she like?"

Dana listened with fascination. The girls were doing his work for him. But at the same time, the board was standing over there frowning at him, and the waves were being blown out by the onshore breeze. Reluctantly he stood up.

"What's she like? Hmm. She's like a brain surgeon," Katie said. "Our house is cleaner than the average test tube. Did you see the towel in front of the door?" she asked Dana.

"Yes. I did notice it."

"Germ trap. Fresh one every day. Catches soil bacteria. And after slobs like you have been to the house, she disinfects the doorknobs."

They laughed, and he saw her smile, as she went on.

"I'm not kidding. When we use the john, we're supposed to spray it with disinfectant. That's in case any of us picked up syphilis from a toilet seat somewhere."

"That's morbid." Annie shuddered.

"A germ that wandered into her bedroom would go into hysterics. I'm serious. But otherwise she's a very nice person. Except that when she eats, she pulls on rubber gloves and says, 'Knife. Fork. Spoon. Clamp!' "

"Hey, I don't want to interrupt," Dana said, "but I've got to try out that board. I'll be back in a half hour or so."

Katie twisted to frown at him. "You're leaving *now?*"

He made a gesture of despair. "The waves are getting blown out. I promised. You could come along—I have to take it up beyond the swimming area. But of course I've got to go out beyond the surf line, so there wouldn't be much point."

Katie lay down again. "No. Not much point," she said.

Annie shot Dana a look that told him, in case he did not already know, that he had blundered.

"No, come on," he said, desperate to sew up the hernia he had created. "We'll find a starfish for Cute- Cunningham."

Katie yawned. *"Machts nichts,* Kapitan," she said. "First things first. Hurry back."

He touched her leg with his toe. "Really, Katie. Come on. You can watch, and when I'm through we'll look for starfish."

"Sorry. Lot of heavy tanning to do. Check with me later. *Adios. Guten tag.*"

Dana lugged the big red board down to the hard sand and walked north beneath the low cliffs. Beyond the waves a dozen surfers roosted on their boards, looking like crows in their black wet-shirts. Damn, damn! He had painted himself into a corner. If he had decided not to try the board after all, it would have made Katie look petulant and spoiled. So he'd had to go through with it; but in doing so, he had alienated her.

Who said chess was intricate?

Well, there was all day to make up for it.

At the surfing flag, he flopped the board down in the shallow water and started wading out. The air was tangy and springlike. Blue-green breakers climbed from the water, sunlight gleaming in the glassy tunnel before them; as they came sliding down, white foam piped their edges. He saw Ruben out there on a white board as slim as a shark. Dana knelt and began to paddle, barged through a few waves, gasping as the cold water broke over him, and joined the other surfers. Ruben paddled over.

"How's it feel so far?" he asked.

"Ever paddle a log?" Dana said. "It's got everything but a lead keel."

"I guarantee it won't tip over. Where's your girl?"

Dana gestured. "On the beach with the others."

"No, I looked as I was riding in, and she wasn't with them."

Dana peered south. Had she been mad enough

to grab a bus and go home? No, no. Gone to the girls' room. Taking a dip.

He wheeled, the nose of the board pointing toward the beach, and started his wave watch. They were coming about every twelve seconds. He tried for a wave, but sloshed out of it, wheeled, and got ready again. Again he missed. He paddled back into position. He saw Ruben riding a wave in, standing tall. Then the Chicano boy suddenly swerved out of it, swung his board, and yelled and waved at the other surfers.

"Somebody in trouble!" he shouted.

Dana looked. All the surfers paddled south to assist the guards in case they needed help. Dana knelt and began to paddle the ungainly board. A hundred yards south, he saw a lifeguard in red trunks splashing through the surf, a red plastic float bobbing behind him.

The rescue was almost complete before he even got close.

The guard had bent a flexible red float around the swimmer's chest, under the arms—it was a girl—her head and shoulders supported above the water. There were surfers all over the place as he started backstroking toward the beach, towing the girl in. She looked totally wet and waterlogged, and made only feeble flapping attempts to use her arms. Dana finally paddled close enough to see her face, and realized with a shock that it was Katie.

15

"You were in a little trouble out there, but you're alright now. Why don't you just lie in the sun for a few minutes?" Dana heard the guard counseling the girl as he ran up. A couple of dozen bathers had gathered. The guard challenged Dana as he knelt beside Katie. "We can handle it, bud."

Dana said, "She's my girlfriend! What happened?"

Katie rolled onto her side and began throwing up salt water and a little breakfast. She moaned and tried to sit up. The guard talked to her.

"You're alright, miss, you didn't swallow much water. Why don't you lie on your face and let the sun warm you?"

Katie was very pale, and shivered in spasms. She was crying. Dana stroked her arm, which felt icy. "Is she okay?" he asked the guard. He was aware of Paul, Annie, and the others standing near him.

"She's a little 'shocky,' but okay," the lifeguard said.

Katie looked as wet and bedraggled as a half-drowned kitten. Her hair was matted. Paul pawed a little sand over the vomit. She looked at Dana, her eyes seeming bleached.

"Oh, boy," she whispered.

He squeezed her hand. "Didn't you have the boogie board?" he asked her.

"No, I didn't think I needed it. I was going to body surf."

Another lifeguard arrived, carrying a clipboard. "How's she doin'?" he asked the first guard.

"She's alright. What's your name, miss?' he asked.

"Katie," she murmured. "Mor-Norman."

Dana gave the guards the rest of the facts. People were drifting away.

"I blew it," Katie said weakly. "I'm sorry."

"God, don't apologize. I shouldn't have left you. But—"

"It wasn't your fault. The waves kept coming, and I couldn't breathe in all the foam, and—"

After she had stopped shivering, Dana led her to the shower pole near the rest rooms and helped her wash off. Then she went into the ladies' room and came out, smiling weakly. "Do you mind taking me home?" she asked.

"I'll get our stuff."

"What happened?" Dana asked the others, at the mats.

Annie said, "I didn't see it happen. She just

kind of disappeared. I know she was mad when you left her alone, though."

"Yeah, I know. But I promised Ruben—I thought she understood."

"She may have understood," Annie said, "but she was hurt." Her eyes were troubled.

Dana rolled up the mats. "Well, I—I sure messed up. Did you guys see it happen?"

Paul shrugged. "She said she didn't need the boogie board, and I saw her walk down to the water. She started swimming out. She didn't look like much of a swimmer, but I didn't really see her get into trouble."

With an armload of gear, Dana asked Annie, "What should I tell her?"

"Butter her up, cowboy," Annie said. "Flattery will get you plenty."

Katie was already wandering back to the car when Dana caught up with her. She trudged along, head bowed, shivering, as he draped a tattered gray beach blanket over her shoulders with one hand.

"You'll warm up pretty soon," he said. "Want to stop and get some coffee?"

"I'd better just go home."

There was a lot he should say, he realized, but he did not know where to start. Certainly he could not mention the talk with Amanda without spilling another pot of beans. He realized that he had never completely bought Amanda's theory of Katie as a potential suicide, despite all the so-called clues. In his mind, a suicidal person remained a cliché figure—despondent, gloomy, anxiety-ridden.

And even if Mrs. Allen was right: Had Katie actually attempted to drown herself, simply because he had been thoughtless?

She surprised him by suddenly taking his arm. "I'm sorry I spoiled your day. I guess I learned something about body surfing, at least."

"You really should have used the board. There's a cord on it to tie onto your ankle, so you can't lose it. Katie, I—I hope—"

She looked at him.

"I know you must have been mad at me. I don't blame you. I got my priorities screwed up. If I thought you went out into the deep water just to show me, I'd feel pretty bad."

He saw her eyes fill, and she sniffled and turned away. "Don't worry, Kapitan. I didn't want to bother with the board, and— All I'm worried about is Marcia." She pawed at her hair, and gave a rueful laugh. "I'm a ruin!"

Dana laid his arm across her shoulders. "What's with this Marcia stuff? Where does your father come in?"

He realized she was crying softly, but after sniffling vigorously and drawing a convulsive sigh, she gave a little laugh.

"Where she leaves off," she said.

16

Katie opened the front door. "Come on in," she said. "I'll make some coffee."

"Thanks." Dana wiped his bare, sandy feet on the bath towel inside the door.

"I'll tell my father I'm back."

Through a glass door Dana could see Mr. Norman lounging on a chaise in the sun, on the sparse lawn. Katie went outside. He sat on the edge of the long leather sofa, a little concerned about super-clean Marcia and the sand between his toes. He had seen her red sports car in the driveway. In the kitchen he heard a young woman laugh, then say, "That'll fix her. See you in the office, Walter. . . ."

He rose as the kitchen door opened. A young woman came through and looked at him blankly. She was small, barefoot, and blond, not much bigger than Katie. Her plaid shirt, rolled to the elbows, looked stylishly casual, and her bleached jeans fit her as snugly as appleskin.

"Hello!" It was put like a question. "You're Kathleen's friend?"

"Yes—if you mean Katie," Dana said. "Dana Furlong."

Marcia looked about. "You're back early, Dana. Where's Kathleen?"

Glancing out the door, Dana saw Mr. Norman rise and take Katie in his arms, patting her back. They started toward the house. Dana gestured.

"She's outside, Mrs. Norman. There was quite a crowd, and we decided to leave. . . ."

"Oh, I see." She had obviously picked up the scent.

Cunningham wandered in, looking sweet and saintly. He took Dana's hand, and Dana smiled but got set to be licked again. And dammit, he had forgotten the starfish!

"Is Katie home?" the little boy asked.

Marcia was watching her husband and stepdaughter, who could have been her younger sister, come onto the red-tiled *saguán*.

"She's coming," Dana told Cunningham.

"What's going on?" Marcia asked in a cool, edged voice, crisp as a rime of ice. "What happened?"

Katie and her father came inside. She was wiping her nose on a man's handkerchief. Mr. Norman said, "Katie got a little waterlogged, Marcia. Why don't you make some coffee?"

Cunningham picked up the situation on his

radar, and began wailing; he plowed into Katie and threw his arms around her. Marcia stood rooted, staring at Katie.

"*Waterlogged?* What's that mean?"

Mr. Norman explained calmly, "There was a rip tide, and Katie got caught in it. No big problem. The guards got to her in plenty of time—"

"Oh, my God," Marcia said. "Little Theater again? Packed house, Kathleen? Audience in tears?"

Dana looked at her, appalled. Marcia appeared intent and somehow excited.

"Cut it out, Marcia," Katie's father said. "Make some coffee, huh? And put a shot of brandy in mine. Couldn't you show a little compassion?"

"I thought you said no big problem?" his wife retorted. "I don't think compassion is the point, I think the point is—*why?* What's going on? Why did she do it?"

Katie put her arms around her brother, and looked at Marcia, her eyes wet and red.

"I didn't *do* anything!" she said. "I got knocked down by a wave. Then I was trying to swim in a lot of foam—"

"That's all it was, Mrs. Norman," Dana said. "It was my fault, I guess, because I left her to try out a surfboard, and she didn't know the surf at Moonlight."

Marcia looked at him coldly. Her eyes were an

eerily pale blue, her lips full, her nose tipped. She looked pretty but a little coarse, without Katie's delicacy. And Dana wondered, as the young woman prepared to unload on him, why he was comparing them, as though somehow they were rivals.

"Dana," she said, "you've come to the show a little late. I won't spoil Act II for you by trying to explain Act I. —Kathleen," she said, "you know how I feel about these spectaculars. Do you realize the effect they're having on Cunningham?"

"Dammit, Marcia," Mr. Norman said, with heat, "I don't think *you* know the effect you're having on *her* by calling her accidents 'spectaculars.' You make it sound as though she were out to get attention."

Marcia gave a sudden sigh, and smiled wearily at him. "I'm sorry, Chuck. But it worries me to have Cunningham upset all the time. And I'm going to have to say—it's worth trying, you'll admit—that until she starts getting her act together, she's to stop babying him—letting him sneak into her bed at night and all that. Just leave him alone for a while, Kathleen. Completely."

Katie walked toward the hall; then Dana heard her bare feet running. Jesus Christ, he thought, staring at Marcia in disbelief. Mrs. Adolph Hitler, I presume? She looked at him quickly, but if she saw his shock and outrage, she was able to ignore them, for she said quietly. "Sorry, Dana. Best of families. I'd invite you to stay for some coffee, but under the circumstances—"

"Sure," Dana muttered. "I'll call her later."

17

On Sunday, Dana raked out all his aviaries, washed down the feeding tables, scrubbed the birdbaths, and checked his nestlings. He was glum and preoccupied. He wanted to call Katie, but had a hunch that he'd better wait until school to talk to her. Things might be going on in that toxic culture Marcia Norman called a family which would make it bad for Katie if he called.

So Cutepig couldn't crawl into her bed anymore. So she was a bad influence on him. Couldn't her father see what Marcia was doing? Taking out some deep-seated disturbance of her own, and maybe a crazy jealousy, on Katie. She was a sickie herself, that seemed obvious, with all her disinfecting.

He had tried to call Mrs. Allen last night, but couldn't reach her. He would try again pretty soon.

Suddenly he realized that his mind, preoccupied as it was with Katie, had made a subconscious note about Nest Box A-7, where his albino nestling was getting ready to go out on its own. He looked again, and found his hunch was right: Its legband had slipped off and become lost in the tangle of torn palm strips. He banded lovebirds at ten or twelve days with closed bands like little wedding rings, which could be slipped on over the small, cartilaginous foot. But if a bird was banded a day or two early, the band might slip off. Too late, and you couldn't get it on.

He would now have to cut a band open and reband it.

After lunch he called Mrs. Allen's number. She answered promptly.

"Dana! Did you try to call me earlier this morning?"

"No, last night."

"Someone called twice, but hung up just as I answered. Well! Tell me all about it."

"Brace yourself, Mrs. Allen. Katie had to be rescued."

"Rescued from what? Oh, darn!" Amanda exclaimed."A crisis?"

"She got out beyond her depth. She was mad at me for leaving her alone, I think, and went swimming by herself to show her independence, I guess."

He recreated the somber happenings of the day.

"I've *got* to get that woman to school," Mrs. Allen sighed. "She sounds like the major part of

Katie's trouble. What about her real mother? Did she talk about her?"

"Not much. I think she had to go into a sanitarium when Katie was nine or ten. TB, she said. No, I really didn't find much out except that Marcia's a mysophobe. That means—"

"Thanks, I believe I know what it means," Amanda Allen said crisply. "She's afraid of germs. Keep after her, Dana. It's important that she knows somebody's really interested in her. With all this anxiety building up, she's got to unload sooner or later."

18

Katie cut classes Monday morning. She installed herself in the library near the art books and leafed through them, half-awake. There was a book on Vincent Van Gogh that fascinated her. She had read his letters and studied his paintings, and knew all the details of his madness and suicide. She was preparing a report, now. She did not understand his cutting off his ear and giving it to a waitress. Now, that was really crazy! But she certainly knew how he had felt when, on that last day, he had used the little pistol to kill himself. He'd had all he could take.

She had felt that way yesterday.

She had gotten up early and left a note on the sink that she was going for a walk. And she had walked! Miles—through lemon groves, macadamia groves, orange groves, and avocado groves. There was something healing about the aroma of earth and blossoms, a living perfume so different from the antibacterial fragrance of home (Marcia's home, not hers).

Was the fragrance part of the miracle that had happened? For in an orange grove she had had an experience that was like an episode from the life of a holy person.

She had gotten hungry, and picked an orange and walked along peeling it. As she drifted through the solemn convention of big, fragrant trees, she had thought about Dana, and Cutepig, and her father; but she had felt strangely as though she were already in an airplane, going somewhere, and they were in the airport busy with boring duties that were important to them but not to her. There was a pearly distance between them. She was outward-bound, sorry-to-leave, glad-to-be-going.

And then, very clearly, she had heard her mother say, *"Hey, it's alright, Katie! You don't have to fight them. Take it easy, like I always did. Don't buy their lies. You don't have to live by anybody's rules but your own. Just keep your mind open and you'll find an answer. Soon!"*

Five minutes later, the answer came to her!

Walking along with her eyes on the ground, she became aware of an enormous tent before her. She raised her eyes and looked at it. It was actually a large gray tarpaulin draped over an orange tree, and there was a sign on it with the word DANGER in red.

Fascinated, she went forward and read the sign. It warned that the tree was being fumigated, and the gas inside the tent was deadly. *"Do not enter under any circumstances."* She recalled reading about derelicts taking shelter for the night under such tents, and being found dead.

The circuitry in her mind slipped channels at that point, and she thought she crawled inside and lay down, using her sweater for a pillow. The fumes smelled slightly of almonds, and it was dim and quiet, like a church. And oh, so restful! Her mother came and smiled at her, but when Katie got up and went toward her, eagerly, she retreated. . . .

And Katie found herself outside once more. Had she actually entered it at all? She guessed not.

But why shouldn't she?

For when she analyzed her life, what was it all about? What did it prove—the suffering, hating herself, and playing pep squadder? Was there a shortage of people or something, that she had to keep going? Whose life was it, anyway?

She raised the skirt of the tent and peered inside. There was an oily, unpleasant odor, and she dropped the canvas quickly. Slowly she walked home, thinking how strange it had been that only a minute or two after her mother had said she would find the answer, she had found it!

Or had she seen it first? And her brain had processed it quickly, knowing what the tent was, so that what was really her own idea had seemed to be a message from her mother.

I'm really getting confused, she thought.

She was reading about the Impressionists that Monday afternoon when a younger student brought her a summons from the office.

"It's from Dr. Warrenton," the boy said, brushing his hair out of his eyes. "The, um, girls' vice-principal."

"I know. Thanks. Am I supposed to tip you?"

"No, but I'll give you a tip," the boy grinned. "Be nice to her. Or you'll be scrubbing toilets."

Katie sighed and left the library. She was barely acquainted with the woman, who was tanned and fit, despite her white hair. She was always friendly, and somehow had learned Katie's name, and spoke when they passed. They said she had special powers with delinquents, which probably described Katie while she was cutting classes.

She gathered her books and walked from the library down to the counseling and English-as-a-second-language wing. She was surprised to see Ruben standing outside a small office waiting to go in.

"Hey, how are you?" he asked. "All dried out?"

She grinned. "Okay! But I sure swallowed a lot of Moonlight Beach Saturday. I hear I lowered the tide six inches."

"What happened?"

"The waves came at me so fast I couldn't get my breath! Wow! And there was so much foam—"

Ruben looked puzzled. "Thirteen-second intervals isn't fast. You'd better take some swimming lessons before you try to body surf again."

"Where's Dr. Warrenton's Office?" Katie asked him.

"Straight down the hall. Are you pregnant or something?"

"No, but thanks for your interest."

A little miffed, Katie went on to the office at the end of the short hall. Temporary-looking desks inhabited by harried workers were randomly arranged in a large area. The clutter and crosstalk reminded Katie of the Motor Vehicles Department when she had taken her driver's license exam. She saw Dr. Warrenton at a desk in a corner. The woman was going through some papers, but saw Katie immediately and beckoned to her, smiling. She looked more like a coach than a counselor.

"Sit down," she said when Katie arrived. She sat back, smiling but intent. There was a plain oak chair beside the desk.

"You haven't been going to many classes today, Katie," Dr. Warrenton said. "What's the matter? Need a Big Sister or something?"

"No, I just haven't been feeling very well."

"Most of us girls don't, at times. There's a cot

in the nurse's office where you can lie down for a while."

"No, thanks, I'm alright."

"All dried out after your Moonlight Beach episode?" The blue eyes were inquisitive.

"Sure." Then, with a little smile, "Who told you about it?"

Dr. Warrenton pondered. "Well, I think one of the hundred or so people on the beach must have been a student, and the student told me. There are no secrets at Moonlight."

"I guess not! It was really just a tempest in a teapot," Katie said.

"People have been known to drown in teapots," Dr. Warrenton said. "If the people are small enough or the pots are big enough. Why don't you enroll in a swimming class and learn how to take care of yourself in the surf?"

"I will."

"Good. That's settled then." Dr. Warrenton didn't believe a word of it, but wasn't pressing. "Where's your mother these days?" she asked.

"She works."

"Every day?"

"Five days a week."

"What does she do?"

"She's the sales manager for a coffee machine service company."

"My gosh," Dr. Warrenton said. "Successful

woman. I was a meter maid till I was forty. Who takes care of your little brother?"

"He goes to a Montessori school."

"How's he doing?"

"I don't know!" Katie laughed, exasperated. "Alright, I guess. I thought you wanted to talk about me."

"My specialty is family life. How's your family life?"

Katie raised and dropped her hands in her lap. "I've only missed a few classes, Dr. Warrenton. I just haven't felt like studying, so I've been reading. But I'm not ditching, so—"

"Right. You're a very good student, and I hope you continue to be. But I think you'll have to show up in classes to pass. By the way, do you have time to do some faculty caricatures for the yearbook?"

"Well, sure—"

"Your art teacher says you've got a fine talent for caricature. See Francis Goodman if you're interested in helping. He's in Journalism right now. And don't forget about that swimming class. They're going on all the time. And if there are any other problems, I'm right here most of the day and I'd be flattered to have a chance to talk to you about them."

Katie got up, fluttered her fingers at her, smiled, and hurried away. And thank *you*,

Amanda Allen, for siccing her onto me! she thought indignantly. You're a busy little bee, aren't you?

19

Monday evening when Dana's mother, dressed to the eyeballs, pulled fish sticks from the freezer, Dana said, "Forget it. I've got a casserole going."

"Oh, thanks, darling," his mother said. "Dad and I have a bridge dinner."

Dana sighed and grated cheese for the tuna casserole, then sliced zucchini for some stir-fry vegetables. He peeled a pear for a salad and concocted a dressing. He felt grouchy. He had seen Katie just before school ended, but when he tried to stop her, she had said, "Marcia's waiting! Mustn't keep her!"

"Katie, listen—!" He felt as though a week had gone by since he'd talked to her. Something had happened that should have made them very close, but she was acting as though they were strangers.

"Later!" she'd said.

With dinner cooking, he went out and sat on the patio, listening to the birds settling in for the night. The chirping and rustling sounds were relaxing.

Wendy wandered out and sat beside him in the dusk, licking flavored lip gloss from her mouth. "What's the matter, genius?" she asked.

"Nothing. You know, you're getting very tall. You'll be ten feet before you're sixteen."

"Blah, blah, blah. At least I don't almost drown."

"Who told you?"

"Ruben called this afternoon."

"Oh. I'll call him later."

"He said he saw Katie Norman going to Dr. Warrenton's office today. Isn't she the parole officer?"

"For Pete's sake! We don't have a P.O. She's the girls' vice-principal."

"Same thing, isn't it?"

"No." But he wondered: Was it related to the fact that she'd cut classes today?

"Maybe she wanted to ask her why she almost drowned."

Dana threw up his hands. "Cut it out! She *didn't* almost drown! She just got out beyond her depth, and a lifeguard dragged her in."

"Why didn't you help her?"

"Because I wasn't there."

"Is she pretty?"

"Very."

"It's funny she picked you for a friend. She's probably just finding her way around the new school."

"Thanks."

Wendy laughed. "Well, you're not exactly romantic. Like leaving her alone on the beach. . . . I'm surprised she even called you."

Dana jumped. "Called me! When?"

Wendy laughed. "Keep cool. I *guess* it was her. Some girl. She wouldn't leave her name. About an hour ago."

"Well, for—! What'd she say?"

"She asked for you, and I said you weren't home yet. She said she'd call again sometime. Sounded kind of sad. . . ."

Dana carried the telephone outside and punched in Katie's number. After three rings, a woman answered.

"Mrs. Norman?" he said. "This is Dana Furlong. I'd like to speak to Katie."

"She's not taking calls this week, Dana."

He grimaced. "Well, I wonder if—"

Click.

Dana racked the receiver angrily. "May your teeth rot in your gums! The tragedy of psoriasis to you, you witch." He kicked a chair. "Her rotten stepmother."

Wendy smeared on some more lip gloss, playing it very cool. "There's some other news."

"Well, come on. Give."

"Did you look at the classifieds this morning?"

"No. Hey, what are you telling me? Not another?"

Wendy picked up a book and extracted the

bookmark, which was about four inches of classified ads.

" 'MUST SELL,' " she read. " 'Blue-masked lovebirds $12.50 apiece. Call after 8:30. 679-0934.' "

"Insane! And that number sounds familiar—I think it's one of the earlier ones."

"What'll you do?"

Dana reflected. "Interesting question. Damn. I do not understand. If she wants to talk, why not call Dial-A-Prayer or something?"

"Maybe she wants to *talk.* Maybe she doesn't want a taped message, or a lecture on not jumping out of windows. Maybe she's rich. And gross. And lonesome. That would be the combination. What's for dinner?"

20

The Lantz kids were in bed—it was eight-twenty—and Katie had already had five responses to her bird ad. She had disconnected the telephone and spread her schoolwork on the coffee table, with the telephone in reach when she wanted to activate it. Amanda Allen had come up with an absolutely crazy assignment today—had *sent* it to her in the library, for Pete's sake!

"LOVE IS . . . (ten different things.)"

Come on, Amanda, she thought: You assigned it to the whole class just to see what I write down! Admit it!

Nevertheless she began to write rapidly:

LOVE IS:

1. When Daddy used to pick me up.
2. When Cutepig crawls into my bed and goes to sleep.
3. A four-letter word.
4. Nothing.
5. Nothing.

6. Nothing.
7. Nothing.
8. Nothing.
9. Nothing.
10. Doing a good caricature.

She finished her homework, put the telephone on the floor beside the sofa, and lay down. Soon it would begin to ring; but she was almost too despondent to play the game. She had placed the ad Friday—along with one for tomorrow morning—when she was feeling so high about the date with Dana.

But now she understood that a Science Major could never understand a loony like the Mysterious Bird Girl. How he had gone on about her! Could she really tell such a boy what had happened in the grove yesterday? He would say it was just coincidence that she had heard her mother's voice a moment before seeing the tent, though she was convinced it had been ESP or something.

The telephone rang; she let it run down like an alarm clock. It rang again two or three minutes later. Finally she picked it up.

"Hmm?" she murmured.

"Uh—I'm calling about the lovebirds you advertised."

It was Dana. She did not reply at once, and he said, "Hello?"

"*Guten nacht,*" Katie said, having decided earlier to hide behind a German accent.

"The birds. Are you German tonight, *fraulein?*"

"*Ja.*"

"Fine. I don't speak German, but maybe you speak a little English. What's the joke this time, *fraulein?*"

"No joke, *mein herr.*"

"You'd better believe it's no joke. In fact, I'm going to call the police tomorrow and tell them about this racket you're running."

"Is no racket." Katie said sadly. "I am secretary for German-American Bird Society. We are wishing to disconnect all our lovebirds—" She stopped, hoping he would break in, because the fun had gone out of the conversation. It had collapsed like a balloon. Now it was like listening to a comedy routine once too often. An awkward silence gathered. Then she heard him speaking, very calmly this time.

"I believe I see through you now, lady. I've done a lot of thinking about you. Would you like to know what I've decided?"

Katie's eyes overflowed. *You'll never see through me, Dana! My future does not include you after all; it consists of two electrodes and a power plant, waiting to blow the craziness out my ears—and the human being called Katie Norman along with it. What did anybody ever do for Van Gogh? Or for Hemingway, for that matter? Or poor, sweet Sylvia.*

But go ahead. Tell me about the Bird Girl.

"I think you go to a private school. That you don't have many friends. Maybe you're lonely, or shy, and certainly overweight. So to make friends, you run these ads. Since that costs money, you must be loaded. What I think you should do is spend some money on a shrink and get off my back. Okay? Because the next time you do it, I'm going to get the SWAT team to smoke you out of the bushes. *Guten nacht, fraulein.*"

"Good night, Dana," Katie said. "I'm sorry about it. I won't do it ever again. This is Katie."

But he must have already hung up, because the only reply she got was the dial tone.

And then she remembered that she had placed another ad for Thursday, too, determined to make Dana play his part in the script she had written. But no problem; she would simply leave the phone off the hook.

21

Dana spotted the ad in the classified columns the next morning. He did not rage; did not snarl; simply accepted the fact that this was the end of the bus line. He and the Bird Girl were getting off. His next move was clear and definite.

Amanda Allen's husband, he knew, was a lawyer. He would ask her to find out from him how to go about getting police cooperation in finding the person who was placing the ad.

But then, eating a bowl of Furlong's Formula with sliced strawberries, he bit his tongue so badly that it bled for five minutes. Pent-up rage went off in his head like a hand grenade.

Oh, the bitch! If I had her alone in an aviary for five minutes—!

With the taste of blood still in his mouth, symbolically, he stormed out to feed the birds. He set the bowls down on the concrete patio so hard that one of them cracked. He swore and had to go to the garage to get another, dumped the greens, apple, meal, and bread into it, and headed toward the aviary at the end of the patio.

Then he saw something, in shock and delight.

Between two peachface lovebirds sat an all-white bird with a black bill. His albino had emerged from the nest-box!

"*Wendy!*" he yelled.

His sister came from the kitchen. "What?"

"My albino's fledged!"

He went to the aviary and stood admiring the little bird between its parents on a manzanita perch. Aside from a slight greenish tinge, which it would lose, the bird was a pure white. One parent was pastel blue, the other green.

"It's pretty," Wendy said. "What's it worth?"

"A million dollars, to me. It's the last step before my True Blue. Oh, damn!"

"What?"

"I've got to reband it. I was going to do it before it fledged. Now I've got to net it. Oh, well—"

Back to the garage. He got a net, and some bands, cut a band open and filed the cut edges smooth, and put it and a pair of needle-nosed pliers in his pocket. Then he slipped into the aviary like a thief.

He talked to the birds, who gathered on a single perch and scolded him. The albino clung to the wire netting. He maneuvered painstakingly, hoping to net it on the first try and not tire it. And there was always the chance of injury when you netted a bird. So, working slowly, he bided his time, then made a pass.

The bird went into the ring and quickly worked itself head-down to the bottom of the cone-shaped net. He drew it out carefully, and examined it. Plump breast-muscle, feet perfect, eyes clear. Feathers glossy. He took up the pliers, the band already in place between the needle jaws. He slipped it over the leg, and—

"Ouch!"

The bird had managed to bite him. It was surprisingly strong. In his momentary pain, Dana closed the leg band clumsily so that the edges did not meet. In fact, he realized as the bird struggled, he had pinched its leg! It squawked in pain. Now he would have to get another pair of pliers and have Wendy help him open the band, and—his finger was bleeding, now.

He thought of the Bird Girl, laughing somewhere as she envisioned the mess she had made of his world.

"Wendy?" he yelled. "Get me a pair of needle-nosed pliers—quick!"

He gasped as the bird sank its little hookbill deeper into his flesh, decided he would have to release it, and opened his hand. But instead of flying to its parents, it headed straight for the translucent plastic of the end wall and tried to fly through it!

There was a small thud.

The bird fell to the floor and lay still.

Dana moaned and closed his eyes. He leaned against a post and listened to himself breathe. He did not want to look. Perhaps it had merely stunned itself. But after a time he opened his eyes. It lay still. He knelt and picked up the small, warm body. Seed hulls clung to the perfect feathers. The little head flopped loosely; there were seed hulls stuck to its ruby eyes. What he held in his hand was only a tiny, cooling handful of down, the end of the line in his long campaign to create a True Blue.

The Bird Girl had won.

22

In a damp sea-fog, Dana parked the moped and climbed to the arched school-ground gate. He was an hour late for classes. Sounds were dulled by the mist, and the campus smelled like freshly-dug earth. Blank-faced, he dumped his books in his locker and plodded toward Mrs. Allen's classroom. Bells shrilled and students began appearing on the walks.

The door to Amanda's room was open, and he went in. Three students were loitering by her desk, their conversation an uninteresting mumble in his ears. ". . . Stanford . . . S.C. . . . three-point-two average . . ." Seniors, discussing college.

"Kids, I have a conference, now," Dana heard Amanda say. "We'll talk later."

The students eyed Dana as they drifted out. He went to the front, dropped into a chair near the teacher's desk, and sighed. She looked at him in some anxiety.

"No more bad news about Katie, I hope?"

"No, no. I haven't talked to the lady again. This is something else. Amanda, it's all over."

"What is?"

"You know I raise birds?"

"I believe I've read some themes on the subject." She smiled in understanding, and waited.

"One of them died this morning."

"Oh, no! I'm so sorry. A special bird?"

Dana got to his feet and began feverishly sketching on the chalkboard what looked like a crossword puzzle, with *X*'s and *Y*'s and certain lowercase letters in each box.

"This is the genetic pedigree . . . of the albino lovebird . . . I just lost," he said, suddenly angry. "The next to the last step in breeding what raisers call the True Blue peachface. It hasn't been bred yet, but my dad's computer tells me this is the bloodline formula for creating it. From this bird I was going to get a True Blue."

"What a disappointment," Mrs. Allen said. "Can you buy another one like it?"

"There isn't another like it! It's taken me four years to reach this point. I could buy another albino for five or six hundred dollars, but I wouldn't know for sure what colors it carried. The parents will eventually produce another albino, but this pair only throws one bird at a time, and the odds against albinos are about ten to one. So I may get nothing but other colors for a couple of years."

"Then all I can suggest," Mrs. Allen replied, "is

patience. And the news that life is no piece of cake."

"My patience," Dana said, "has run out. Now I want revenge."

She snorted. "Oh, Dana. Against fate?"

"Against the Mysterious Bird Girl."

"The Who?" Amanda laughed. "Dana, you're hallucinating."

He related the saga of the Bird Girl.

"And today," he finished, "there was another ad in the classified. I've got to find her, shame her, scare her, whatever it takes to make her understand that I mean business. I thought maybe your husband could tell me how to start."

Amanda tipped back in the chair and contemplated him seriously. "Are you sure you want to meet her?"

". . . Of course!"

"What if it's an emotionally disturbed person placing the ads?"

"Then she's got to be stopped for her own good, not to mention the bird world's. If she's disturbed—well—she can get treatment after she's been stopped."

Amanda crossed her arms. "It's an old dilemma, Dana—where punishment ends and treatment begins. But I suppose it's up to you. Ever hear of the Upside-Down Book?"

He frowned. "Sounds like a child's garden of verses."

"It's a telephone directory that gives the numbers first, and then the addresses. The police have them, and so do most libraries. You could call the downtown library and ask them to look it up for you."

Dana stood up slowly, carbonation fizzing in his veins. "Hot dog!" he said. "Really?"

Amanda raised her hand like a traffic cop. "Yes, but wait a minute, my friend. Human beings are fantastically complicated. A computer is a toy compared to the human psyche. Think about it before you rush in. Maybe if you simply quit answering, she'd quit running the ads."

"You forget one thing, Amanda. She owes me at least five hundred bucks for that bird. If I hadn't been upset by the ads, I wouldn't have bungled a simple job like banding a bird. She needs to know that. Oh, boy!" He chortled. "It's my turn!"

23

Katie was pitching, Dustin Barnum was trying to hit the plastic ball, and Jill was doing gymnastics on the lawn. It was Friday night, and almost dark in the Barnum's backyard. Katie's mind kept slipping out of gear, greased by anxieties as intangible as ghosts. Last night she had awakened several times hearing a hammer pounding. But each time she had realized that the pounding was the beating of her pulse in her ears. It worried her. Did she have high blood pressure?

She laughed every time one of the children spoke, and that seemed to satisfy them. But her mind was on the Palomar grade.

"It looked like she missed the guardrail on purpose," Dana said to the patrolman. "I was following her on my moped, and all of a sudden she just hung a right—"

Another officer was going through her purse. "I see she was a member of the pep squad at Santo Tomas High," he said, reading one of her membership cards.

"Judging by all these pictures, she must have had a lot of friends—"

"She did," Dana agreed. "And yet—I don't know—"

"Katie!" Jill's voice said. "I said I hurt my ankle doing a walkover, and you laughed!"

She landed, slightly dazed. "I'm sorry. Did you go to the nurse?"

"Yes, and she put some tape on it."

"Well, you'd better take it easy. Hey, time to eat, you guys! I'll put the chicken in the freezer."

"Not the *freezer,* Katie, the microwave," Dustin laughed.

"Whatever," Katie said.

"Why is she wearing a cheerleader's outfit?" asked the doctor.

"They're supposed to wear tham all day whenever they have practice," Dana said.

"Well, I don't know how she could demolish the car so completely and not get a mark on her body," said the doctor.

The young woman in the granny gown said sadly, "Her body was always so perfect except for that little birthmark. It used to bother her when I'd make fun of it. I suppose I shouldn't have."

"Who are you?" a cop asked.

"Her real mother."

Dustin tugged at her arm, and she laughed and hugged him, then got the chicken out of the oven. Jill had set the table. It was after eight before they finished eating. She had disconnected the telephone earlier, and would leave it disconnected. Suddenly Jill said, "Know what?"

"No, what?"

"After you were here last week, Daddy got a bill for a classified ad! He had to call the newspaper and tell them it was a mistake."

"Weird," Katie said. "I'm sure it won't happen again."

None of it would happen again, in fact. Dana had been a dream. She had loved him, and thought he could help her. But only a sick person could understand another sick person's fears, and *they* couldn't help anybody. Who could she help, for instance?

But she had this strange and exciting hope, now, that her mother was coming back to help her. God knows *she* was sick enough to understand! Had the message in the grove been her first communication? Was her mother dead, now, and trying to return? It was exciting to think about.

With the children in bed, she settled herself at Mr. Barnum's desk and began her homework.

A few minutes later the doorbell chimed. She capped her pen and walked toward the entry, rehearsing her instructions. Ask their name, Katie, but don't let anyone in. Just tell them to leave a message. You can see visitors through the eyepiece. In case of emergency, hit any button on the burglar alarm panel.

She turned on the porch light. "Who is it?" she said into the grille.

"Rosie Caborca," said a boy's voice. "Anne-Marie. Belle, from Trinidad."

She went lightheaded and breathless. He had found her! But now she realized how hopeless and cruel the whole scheme had been, what a fantasy. And she had no idea how to explain it without giving away the fact that she was sick.

She opened the door, and he looked at her in shock.

They sat among the deep chairs in the living room. Dana, wearing a sweatshirt with LOVE IS A FOUR-LETTER BIRD printed on it, and ragged denim shorts and sandals, regarded her in a dazed way. He carried a small white florist's box.

"I don't believe this," he said. "You?"

Katie looked down at her lap. Her tongue clung to the roof of her mouth like a Band-Aid, and she could not catch her breath.

"It was you, Cheers?" he said.

She nodded, without looking up.

"This isn't happening," Dana said. "Oh, wow." He gazed around the room, as if looking for someone to share his disbelief.

"I'm sorry," Katie said in a whisper.

He was almost panting, as if he had sprinted all the way, though he had ridden over on his moped. He struck his brow like a silent-film actor. "Man, this is it! You have arrived at the center of the universe. Do not touch the Bird Girl, or the universe will collapse. Got anything to drink, Cheers?"

She bounced up. When I come back from the kitchen, I will apologize, very formally. I will tell him good-bye. He is a nice boy I have been mean to, but there is nothing between us but pollywogs and lab write-ups.

"Cola or what?" she asked, looking at her feet.

"Surprise me." Then he laughed and struck his brow again, realizing, she supposed, that she had just handed him the ultimate surprise of his life.

In the kitchen she had to sit down, sniffle a little, and wipe away a few tears; then she blew out her breath and got up quickly. She opened a soft drink and poured it with a shaking hand into two glasses, with ice cubes, and carried them back. Fascinated, Dana watched every move she made. She sat down, her knees together, eyes averted. Dana drank some cola and shook his head.

"What are you doing here?" he asked. "Whose house is this?"

"I'm baby-sitting."

"Where are the kids?"

"In bed. Dana, I'm very sorry that—"

"So all this time," he said, roughshod, "you've been chuckling behind Das Kapitan's back. I suppose you'd tell your jock friends every morning after you'd made a fool of me?"

"No!" she cried. "Nobody knows but me."

Dana drank some more cola, rattled the ice cubes, scrutinized her, then sank deeper into the chair. "I don't read you, Katie. What was the point? To watch me go bananas? Lose my shirt? I lost a very nice bird this morning, lady, because of my lousy state of mind."

Katie closed her eyes and started speaking, hoping that if she did not look at him she could explain a morsel of it.

"I . . . wanted . . . to talk to you . . . about—some things," she said, then realized suddenly that she could not say it.

"What things?"

"Nothing. Why don't you leave?"

To her surprise, he suddenly said, "Yes, there is something and I'll forgive you if you'll tell me why you did it."

She risked a look into his eyes; he was smiling in sympathy. He had changed tack, or something. Aha! He was beginning to pry, like Mrs. Allen, or Dr. Warrenton. He was an honorary member of the electroshock goon squad!

"I used to do it at my other school," she said mechanically. "It was fun. To hear people steam up . . ."

Then, dammit, she felt the tears flowing down her cheeks!

"No, Katie," he said, rising and walking toward her. "That wasn't it. What's the problem?"

"There is no problem! I'm just a stupid little cow who likes to play tricks. I keep a diary about tricks I play on people. Go home, dummy!"

He laid a hand on her shoulder, but she twisted away. "Hey, Katie," he said. "It's me, St. Dana. I'm here to talk about your problems."

She tore away from him, screamed, "Oh, don't be so forgiving! Go change some water into wine, St. Dana! I'm not supposed to have any guests, so get out."

Dana shrugged. "Okay, okay! But I want to talk about this tomorrow, after we've both slept on it. I think you owe it to me."

"Alright!"

After he left, she saw that he had left the florist's box by his chair. She opened it, and shuddered when she saw a small dead bird, white except for a black bill. She closed it quickly and put it in the trash-compactor.

When Mr. Barnum took her home, she found that Marcia was still at the home of some friends. Katie's father had had to fly to Honolulu yesterday for an educators' conference. Marcia had taken Cutepig with her and put him to sleep at her friends'.

Poor little boy, she thought. *I wish I could take him with me.*

She changed into her white nightgown and went to her stepmother's private bathroom. There was a small bottle of yellow tranquilizers in Marcia's medicine chest, a red sticker on it warning against taking the drug in combination with alcohol, or before operating machinery. Okay—no machinery, she agreed. She drew a glass of water (drinking out of Marcia's own glass, hoping the witch caught something) and swallowed all the banana-colored tablets in two gulps. Then she brushed her hair thoroughly, and let it flow like silk over her shoulders. She put on some of Marcia's flame-red lipstick, and blue eye shadow. She wanted to study her reflection in the full-length mirror, but for some reason she could not look at herself.

In the kitchen, she found a fifth of Wild Turkey, and poured herself a drink, half liquor and half sweet mixer. She went to her room and dug out a large color photograph of herself that her father had insisted on having made when last year's class pictures were taken. She went to the living room, already groggy with pills and alcohol, propped the picture on a coffee table, and lay on the couch.

She had meant to write a letter to her father, but she was too sleepy now.

Although she was crying a little, she felt warm

and safe. Ever since her mother had left she had been slaving over that terribly complicated equation she had felt she had to solve, each factor in it consisting of hundreds of subfactors, some expressed in fractions, some in decimals, so that to perform a simple function like going to the beach, she had to work out pages and pages of intricate problems. But the joke, which she had finally caught onto, was that she didn't have to solve it! She could simply drop out, as her mother had.

So that was what she was doing.

You didn't have to be popular.

People didn't have to admire you.

You could be scared; it didn't matter.

You didn't have to achieve anything.

You could just quit and float away.

Beautiful.

24

Dana had looked forward with anxiety to seeing Katie on Friday, but she was not at school. And of course he could not call her at home. By Saturday he was in torment. He had to talk it over with someone, so he called Amanda Allen. But the phone rang in an empty house.

Savagely he raked the aviaries, driving the birds crazy with that and other make-work projects to keep his mind off Katie. He had walked out of the house where she was baby-sitting with a clear, disturbing realization that she needed help for sure. Mrs. Allen was right. In fact, he realized, she had probably suspected that it was Katie behind the bird ads the minute he told her, and that was why she had advised him to go easy on the culprit.

He started to dial Paul, but hesitated. Paul was level-headed, might have some idea of what to do. But he had promised Amanda not to repeat what she had said.

The hell with it! he decided, reaching for the

telephone again. He did not have to tell about his conversation with Amanda. He would simply tell him about Katie and the ads.

Paul answered promptly. "Are you busy?" Dana asked.

"No. Francis is here. He wants to hear his new record on my set-up. Can you come over?"

"I'm leaving right now."

Paul's house was on Crest Drive, above a little vale of flower farms. Though it was only a half mile from the ocean, the view was of the mountains twenty miles east. The front door was open when Dana walked up the drive, and he could hear Jamaican reggae music. Paul's room was downstairs, and after glancing around the living room he went on down.

Paul stood in the middle of his bedroom, being assaulted by music from arrays of speakers. He beckoned to Dana. "Stand right here and you'll feel the bass in your gut!"

"I feel something in my gut," Dana said. "Hi, Francis."

The editor was sitting on Paul's bed, which had a fake leopard-skin cover. "Funny," he said, "the record never sounds this good at home. The treble's kind of muffled. Should I get tweeters?"

"Tweeters, tweeters!" Paul said. "Everybody wants to solve all his problems with tweeters. The fact is, they have very little effect on the upper middle range, which is where your problem is—"

"My friends," Dana said, "my problem is that I need to talk. Turn down the music, will you? I don't want to shout this stuff. It should be whispered, at best."

Paul cut the music to a throbbing murmur, and Dana leaned against the wall and looked at them. "I've found the Bird Girl," he said.

Paul cheered.

"Lemme guess!" Francis cried, rising quickly. "A—let's see—young Navy wife, alcoholic, husband at sea. Does it as a joke."

"No, no—a girl in a mental institution," Paul guessed. "Takes the calls on the pay phones."

"Pretty close, but hang on, now," Dana said. "And please don't pass it on."

"Somebody we know?" Paul sounded awed.

"Katie," Dana said.

Paul's grin faded. "Katie Norman?"

Francis sat down, abruptly. *"Katie?"*

Dana gazed out the window. "A very strange deal. I know a little more about her than I can tell, but I would say there is something sick *chez* Norman. Katie's been making the calls as a joke, she says. But I don't believe it."

"Well, then, why?" asked Paul. "Katie? No . . .

"How'd you find out?"

"Amanda gave me a tip on tracing telephone

numbers. Katie'd use numbers where she was going to baby-sit. That way the ads didn't cost her anything. But of course her customers were bound to get onto her. It was screwy."

"But why did she do it?" Francis asked.

Dana touched one index fingertip with the other. "*First* she said she did it as a joke. *Then* she said she'd wanted to talk to me about some things. *Finally* she said she *didn't* want to talk. My guess is that she did, and she was attracting my attention. Though she'd already done that. God, I don't know! And I don't know why she needed to run two more ads after we went to the beach."

Paul studied him, his face grave. "What kind of problems *chez* Norman?"

"Her stepmother is cruel and unusual, in my opinion. I think that's the basis of Katie's trouble."

"What *is* her trouble?"

"I'm not supposed to tell. Amanda Allen's secret."

The telephone rang, and Paul answered. "Dana?" he said. "Yeah, he's here. Just a minute."

He offered the telephone to Dana. "It's Ruben. Wendy told him you were here."

Dana sat on the floor with the phone. "What's up?"

"This is kind of personal," Ruben's voice said. "My sister told me, and she said it shouldn't go any farther. A kind of medical ethics thing."

A little gnat of worry began to buzz in Dana's head. "That's your married sister?"

"That works at the hospital. She was on duty in the emergency room Thursday night. . . ." A pause. A cold handful of fingers began sorting through Dana's bowels. ". . . And about midnight Katie Norman's mother brought her in. They had to pump out her stomach. She'd taken some pills and whiskey. I thought I should tell you, since you're a good friend of hers."

"Yeah, right. Well, uh—is she in the hospital?" Dana seemed to view himself from farther off, a responsible, steady young man sitting on the floor receiving disastrous news as coolly as a general.

"No, they let her go home. She's okay. It was just tranquilizers, Helen said."

"Yeah. Hey, thanks a lot, Ruben. I'll keep it to myself."

He replaced the handset and lay back, in the bent-knee situp position, gazing at the wall.

"Somebody sick?" Paul asked.

"It was about Katie. But let's keep it to ourselves. She had an accident—or something—with pills and booze. Night before last, after I'd gotten on her case."

There was a silence, almost one of embarrassment. Paul came over and nudged Dana with his toe. "Well, listen, buddy. It wasn't your fault, so don't start blaming yourself."

"I didn't help much," Dana said.

"I didn't realize she was into booze or drugs," Francis said.

Dana looked at them. "I guess there's no reason to keep Amanda's confidence any longer, since it's leaked out anyway. But don't repeat this, will you? She thinks she's suicidal. That's why I asked her to go on the beach party. I thought she was wrong, but then when Katie had the swimming accident, I wondered. And now . . ."

"The suicidal cheerleader?" Francis said thoughtfully. "It's a contradiction in terms."

"How was she when you left that night?" Paul asked. "Did she give any indication—?"

"She was about half hysterical, I guess. But she promised to talk with me about the ads again. Then she practically threw me out. Maybe she drank some whiskey to feel better, and tossed down a couple of pills. . . . No, it doesn't hang together," Dana said. "Because she has a bad driving record, too, and the drowning thing. And I read a poem she wrote about dying in a Porsche. She does book reports on suicides, too, Amanda says."

"Why doesn't she have counseling?" Paul asked. "It's ridiculous. What's wrong with her parents?"

Dana said, "That's the big question. Her stepmother is a killer, and her father seems a little passive. And Katie won't talk to anybody. So Mrs. Allen asked me to try to help. St. Dana, as Katie calls me. I can't say I've passed any miracles so far. But maybe after this Amanda will be able to drag Katie and her stepmother in for a conference."

"What are you going to do now?"

"I don't know. I'm not going to drop out. She picked me to help her, I think. . . ."

Paul smiled wryly, and kicked him gently. "Stand by your woman, St. Dana," he said.

25

"You know the next step, don't you, Kathleen?" Marcia said, tooling the Porsche into the school parking lot on Monday afternoon. Loaded yellow school buses were pulling out, snorting and smoking. Kids on bikes, motorcycles, and mopeds were leaving. The scene looked like the Redcoats were coming.

"I won't see a psychologist, if that's what you mean," Katie muttered.

"That's not what I mean." There was a special timbre to Marcia's voice, a fierce imperative like that of a police siren. "I mean a foster home, a parolee house—a nuthouse, maybe. Or electroshock. I won't have my son subjected to your fits of drama every week."

Katie squeezed her eyes shut. "What did my father say?" she asked. They had parked in a red zone, and Marcia was brutally whipping a comb through her hair, then giving it a shake.

"I couldn't reach him."

"Don't you have the name of the hotel where he's staying?"

"He said he'd call us when he got located. He couldn't get reservations in Honolulu before he left."

Liar! Katie thought.

"Now, listen. I'm going to handle this so you won't have to go into an institution or something. You realize that an institution is a very real possibility?"

Her heart pounding, Katie said, "I'd run away!"

"Well, you don't have to, if you back me up. Who is this 'Amanda Allen' busybody, anyway?"

"Just my English teacher. The one who tried to get you to come in before. She does counseling, too."

Marcia got out. "Straighten your hat—up off your face more."

Katie was interested in the prospect of a clash between Mrs. Allen and Marcia. She sensed that the teacher could be as tough as her stepmother, though Marcia had the advantage of not caring a damn about the truth. Katie led the way toward Mrs. Allen's room, Marcia staying beside her with fast, hard-heeled little strides. Katie noticed boys looking at her stepmother as they passed; Marcia was pretty and shapely and made the most of her B-cups. She had instructed Katie in what to wear today—the turned-up brown hat, for innocence; a pink blouse for sweet sixteen; and a brown skirt for stability. Nothing complicated here. Nobody here but us loonies, warden. Katie had been glad to cooperate. Anything to stay out of custody!

When they entered, Katie saw that Amanda had dressed for the occasion, too—a white turtleneck sweater and a navy skirt. She looked very cool and professional, and her long dark hair glistened.

"Thank you for coming, Mrs. Norman," she said. "Hi, Katie. Let's all sit right here. I'll close the door."

Katie sat down, and Amanda returned from the door to sit beside her and squeeze her hand, while Marcia remained warily on her feet, like a boxer. The hand-squeeze nearly did Katie in. She choked up and almost sobbed. Mrs. Allen really likes me, she thought. What would happen if I blurted it all out? Well, one thing that would happen would be custody, as Marcia said.

"Would you mind telling me what this is all about?" Marcia asked, with icy disdain.

Mrs. Allen regarded her intently. "You honestly don't know?"

"If it's about Katie's accident, you're wasting everyone's time. There's nothing to discuss."

"You don't call attempted suicide worth discussion?"

Marcia sat down, crossed her arms furiously, and stared at the teacher. "Mrs. Allen, I told you over the telephone that it was an accident! Shall I write it on the board?"

"No, Mrs. Norman, and please don't get sarcastic. We're talking about Katie's well-being, and that's not a subject for cheap shots. Will you tell me how you can possibly construe this as an accident?"

Katie smiled dreamily at Amanda. Pretty good! she thought. She had hooked Marcia into a full discussion, now.

"Katie baby-sat Thursday night," Marcia said, in a tone of mock patience with someone very dull. "She was upset over some schoolwork when she left the house, and the children upset her still more. She was nervous, that's all. Isn't that so, Katie?"

"Yes. I felt kind of sick." She put a hand on her stomach.

Amanda winked at her. Katie looked away.

"And when she got home I wasn't there, so she had no one to talk it out with, and decided to take one of my Valiums. And for good measure—like a lot of adults, by the way—she took two. . . ."

"Then I decided to drink some of Daddy's bourbon to hurry the pills up," Katie volunteered. "And I guess the combination of pills and whiskey upset me, because then I got *terribly* nervous, really bananas! and I decided to take a couple more. It was crazy!" She laughed. Marcia frowned at her in warning. She realized she was overdoing it, and immediately settled down.

"And wound up taking twenty-two?" asked Amanda. "That's what the hospital estimates they pumped out of you. You've accounted for four pills and a shot of bourbon, but we still have eighteen pills to account for."

"What you're saying," Marcia interrupted, "is that Katie is suicidal. Did she look suicidal when she walked in here just now? She was smiling."

"Katie can't help smiling. It's like hiccups—cheerleader's syndrome. That's what I'm saying, Mrs. Norman. That there's a lot going on beneath the surface. By the way, why didn't Mr. Norman come with you?"

"He's in Honolulu, on business."

"Have you telephoned him?"

Marcia expostulated, "Will you *please* stop going on like this? There are accidents, and accidents, and Katie had one of a kind she won't repeat. And by the way, there were sleeping pills in the medicine chest, too, if she'd really been thinking of suicide."

Mrs. Allen's brows went up. "Did you see them, Katie?"

"Yes." She had seen the red capsules, and was not sure why she had taken the tranquilizers instead. Marcia had a good point about the "accident." The only trouble was, it wasn't true.

"And why didn't you take them?"

"Well, because—I didn't want to kill myself!" Katie said, with a little laugh of incredulity. (Kill myself! What nonsense.)

"You just wanted to come close," said the teacher. "So that someone would help you to get your head straight. Isn't that right? It was a cry for help."

Marcia stood up. "Well, your theorizing is beyond me, Mrs. Allen. If there was anything amiss, I suspect it was because you've been piling on the work beyond her ability to keep up. Is that my fault? It seems to me that schools are trying to shift their responsibility to the parents. If you can't handle the kids, you come whining to us."

"I'm not hearing this," said Amanda Allen. "Katie had an 'accident,' and it's our fault here at school?"

"What do you have counselors for? Aren't they supposed to stay tuned in on the kid's state of mind?"

"Exactly! But Katie hasn't let us help her. I suggest that you get her started on some psychotherapy, immediately—tomorrow. I can recommend a woman near here. She's helped suicidal students in the past. Katie's not the first, by any means. I suppose you know suicide is the main cause of death among teenagers?"

"No, and I don't believe it. Come on, Kathleen," Marcia said.

Amanda took a business card from her desk and handed it to Katie. "This is the woman I mentioned. The next time you feel too depressed to live, call her. I've already mentioned you to her. You won't even have to talk. Just say your name, and she'll talk to you. Could anything be easier than that?"

She put her arm around Katie's shoulders and gave her a hug. Katie's eyes flooded, and she sobbed aloud, crumpled the card in her hand, pulled away, and walked quickly to the door.

They walked back through the almost-deserted campus. At the car Marcia said, "Give me that card."

"I dropped it in a trash barrel," Katie said. But she still had it crumpled in her hand. It felt so good to cheat on Marcia! After she was in the car, she crushed it down behind her in the upholstery. She sniffled a little to keep her nose from running.

"Oh, don't make a soap opera out of it," Marcia said in exasperation.

"I'm not! Why don't you stay off my case?" Katie flared. "You leave me alone, and I'll leave you and your precious son alone."

Marcia, starting the car, stared at her in surprise, then laughed. "Well, aren't we the little smart-ass today?"

"You think you're so—so good! So capable and everything. . . ."

"Yes, I think I'm pretty good," Marcia said. "I don't have much pity for whiners, if that's what you mean."

"Cutepig's a whiner," Katie said.

"Alright, Kathleen! One more remark about Cunningham, and I'll have you in a halfway house so fast it'll make your head spin."

"No, don't—I love him, but he needs a lot more love. He always has, and that's why he sneaks into my bed."

"You let me worry about Cunningham, sister, and you worry about yourself. There seems to be plenty to worry about. You'd be in a padded cell right now, if I hadn't handled this right."

"Oh, stop it!" Katie sobbed, putting her hands over her face and bending over until her face rested in her lap.

Marcia drove fast, across Crest Drive and down the hill to Camino Real, north along the highway between two ridges, then east on the winding road into the hills. Katie sat back wearily, the wind calming her. It was almost like her fantasy of driving down the Palomar Observatory grade. She looked at the leather-wrapped steering wheel, and a sudden realization took her breath. It would take only one quick pull on the wheel, at this speed, to make the car flip! Her heart went crazy with excitement, and her ears stiffened like a cat's.

Then Marcia looked at her, frowned, and said,

"Get a cigarette out of my purse and light it for me, will you?"

" 'Kay," Katie said.

When she handed over the lighted cigarette, her heart was beating normally again. There remained only a lurid shadow of smoking flares, a red car, and bloody stains on the blacktop.

"It's hard to believe they were in the same car," the young doctor said, tossing a canvas sheet over Marcia. "The woman's just hamburger, but there isn't a mark on the girl's body."

"I think I know her," the highway patrolman said. "My son plays football at Santo Tomas High, and she's a cheerleader. I'd almost swear . . ."

"Yes—her name's Katie Norman," a boy among the disaster sightseers said. "I took her out once."

"Then why didn't you help her?" the leftover hippie lady said, from the edge of the road.

"She's your daughter; why didn't you?" Dana retorted.

They got to arguing about who was responsible and Katie smilingly dreamed on, knowing it did not matter, that she was the captain of her fate anyway.

26

Katie was not in biology on Monday. Dana did not see her until Tuesday morning, and that was at a distance. But she was in her blue-and-white cheerleader outfit, so he knew she had practice after school.

"I'll catch her there," he told Paul and Francis, in the cafeteria.

"Can you talk there?" Paul asked.

"No, but I can ask for a date. Something special. I don't know what, yet."

"Tell you what," said Francis. He dug a key from his pocket and laid it beside Dana's plate. "That would be special."

"The key club! Sensational!" Dana said. "Take her to dinner, and then—"

"Remember, though, it's *verboten*. Thursday would be better than Friday, because too many people use it Friday. After nine, on Thursday, you should have it all to yourselves."

Dana clutched the key like a talisman.

"Think you should clear this with Mrs. Allen?" Paul asked.

"I did. I said I wanted to take Katie out to dinner and give her a chance to open up a little. She said, Great idea!"

After school he found her. She was among the cheerleaders on the basketball court, everybody in blue and white, screaming, clapping, and jumping. She looked as good as new, healthy and happy; Katie recycled. No wonder people could not believe she was not perfectly normal! But last week had made a believer out of him.

At the first break, she acknowledged she had seen him with a little wave. He beckoned to her vigorously, but she shook her head. When he started toward her, she laughed and trotted to meet him.

"Hi! How're you doing?" she asked.

Amazing! he thought. The safe deposit vault where she lived was impregnable. "Fine. How about you?"

"Oh, I'm the best, as you can see," she said, and clapped. But there were fine lines, like scratches on silverware, around her eyes.

"Still under house arrest?"

"Yeah!" she said, in disgust. "Because of my dumb accident."

He reached for her hand. She tried to tug it away at first, but then let it go limp as a fish. "I've got a lot to tell you, Katie," he said. "Both before and after the ads. But I can't do it on the campus, can I?"

"I don't know. Can't you?"

"No. So we'll have to go someplace intimate, like the Trident, for dinner, on Thursday."

"Oh, nice," she said. "But no can, my friend. Barbed wire, watchtowers, and dogs. I only go out now for baby-sitting work."

Little pulleys raced and stuttered in his head. "When they pick you up," he said, "do they come in the house?"

"Not usually. They just honk, or ring the doorbell, and I go out."

"*Voilá!* I honk, you come out. What a dirty trick to play on Marcia. She thinks you're baby-sitting, and you're stuffing yourself on seafood, in the arms of the man you love. Well—the man you like."

Katie's laugh trilled. But then, "Oh, Dana, I can't. You want to get me executed?"

"If that's the only way to get you in my clutches."

"You! I was warned—seven-thirty?" she asked.

Dana's head swam. "You will?"

"Yes. I'd love it."

"And listen," he whispered, "wear a swimsuit under your, um, outer garments."

"Swimsuit? I don't know about you," Katie said, eyeing him. But then she laughed again, said, "Okay, Kapitan!" and ran back to the pep squad.

27

Your real mother.

Marcia . . . mysophobia.

Auto accidents.

It was late Thursday afternoon. In his room Dana was laboring over the questions he wanted to ask Katie. Or *thought* he should ask her—he had such a feeble grasp of how to burglarize her mind. He tried to commit the items to memory, but got upset over which ones had priority, and finally gave up the whole investigative-reporter approach. He was trying to make an instrument landing on a desert landing strip. Let it happen, man, let it happen!

With a desperate look at the clock, he realized he had gone overtime on the research. Hurriedly he threw clean clothes on the bed and went to shower.

He dressed in a sport shirt, tan slacks, sneakers, and a sweater. Towels! As he was getting them from the linen closet, Wendy poked her head out of her room.

"What're the towels for?"

He gave a guilty start, then glared at her in fury. "We're going to smear each other with mud, and then wash it off," he said.

"Romantic," she said. "Is that how people make love?"

"Knock it off! And keep quiet."

"I hope you know what you're doing."

"I do."

The Chevy or the Audi? Either way, he would have to ask for the keys. And they would inquire about the towels, unless he stowed them in the car first. But they were playing bridge hands in the kitchen, and would see him going into the garage.

Okay, the Audi, and try to bluff it out.

Carrying the towels, tightly rolled, he sauntered into the kitchen. His father was studying his bridge hand, a big, florid man with prematurely white hair, very impressive on the platform and a terror to his lab assistants. He looked up, preoccupied over a bid.

"Going out?" he said.

"Yeah. I told you—Kathleen Norman, dinner, blah, blah, blah. Can I take the Audi?"

His father dug for his keys. His mother gave him a vacant, fond, smiling regard.

"What're the towels for, blah, blah?" asked his father.

"Maybe we'll go for a swim."

"Is this the girl—?" his mother began, looking troubled. Of course Wendy had spilled it last week, and he had had to explain about the surf accident.

"El mismo—la misma," he said, catching the keys his father tossed. "But we're not going for a night swim in the Pacific Ocean, Mom, so don't worry. If we go, it will be in Francis's pool—the condo pool."

"Crack that calculus problem?" asked his father sternly, picking up his cards.

Dana shook his head. "I'll try it again in the morning. I need a break from it. It's like one of those problems you told me about once, where there's an 'imaginary number' involved, and if you look at it, it will disappear like spots before your eyes."

His father laughed. "I don't think you've looked at this one long enough for it to disappear. I'll go over it with you tomorrow night."

"No, hon, the big doings at the Brittners', remember?" Dana's mother said. "Chance for some red points."

"Oh, of course. Better if you work it out yourself anyway," Dana's father muttered, sinking into the swamp of suits, red and gold points, and kings and queens and trumps.

Dana's ears rang with excitement as he backed the Audi into the street.

Out in the country the darkness was perfumed with the promise of summer. A few early moths fluttered in the beam of the headlights. Near Mockingbird Farms a little coyote loped across the road. Bill St. John told of hawks actually diving against the wire of his aviaries, trying to nail his birds. Dana loved it out here, and someday, when he had saved some money, he would—the dream went—buy four acres and start building cages. . . .

According to the illuminated clock on the dashboard, he was pretty close to schedule. At this instant, Katie might be brushing her hair! Exciting thought; he imagined the sensuous whisper of the bristles, hoped she would let her hair fall to her shoulders as she sometimes did. It was sexy.

He parked at the intersection of the County Road and Old Stage Road, which was Katie's, letting the clock run out. He was getting hives inside his stomach, and needed to scratch them. He felt as panicky as a valedictorian who had forgotten his notes.

One minute before he was due, he restarted the engine and made the final approach through the citrus groves to the high ground where she lived. The house was sprinkled with lights. He coasted down the crunching granite drive, parked, hesitated before honking.

"That doesn't sound like their horn to me, Kathleen. . . ."

His nerves contorted in agony as the horn ruptured the darkness. He waited. Thirty seconds later the door opened, light splashed the slats of the porch, and Katie ran out in a sweater and skirt.

28

"And with a little bit of luck," Katie said, as they drove through the perfumed night of the groves, "I'll be home free and she'll never know. God, I love to cheat on her!"

"Funny lady, that," Dana said. "Can you play with Cutepig yet?"

"The cold war continues. How come Thursday instead of Friday?"

Dana reached for her hand, but it eluded him, like a trout. "I couldn't wait for Friday."

"You're beginning to sound like a jock," Katie said.

"For me, that's progress," Dana said. "Also, Thursday is a better night for what we're going to do than Friday."

"Aha. The bikini bit. But if you think I'm going in that rotten ocean again—!"

"I don't, Kathleen. No way."

"How'd you know my name was Kathleen?"

"I heard Marcia use it. The day you ran the cherryhead ad . . ."

"Mmmm." He had hoped it would lead to something, but all it led to was a thoughtful silence. Then she said, as though musing aloud, "I think of your parents as big social people. Lots of parties, but maybe lemonade instead of booze. Climbers. Religious."

"You're describing Marcia, aren't you, except the religion?"

"Maybe. Do they know you're out with me?"

"Sure. I had to tell them, to get the car."

"What did they say?"

"Mom said, Four spades."

She giggled. "What?"

"They play bridge like W. C. Fields drank gin. But I ran a finesse by them tonight—had to, you see, when they saw the towels."

"If they aren't like Marcia, what are they like?" she persisted.

Dana was aware that the wrong person was asking the questions, but it was a beginning.

"Good people, honest and hardworking—if you call bridge working. My dad fed some bridge problems into a computer at the plant. Sometimes when they think he's brooding over theme and variations on some bug, he's really pondering whether to give a jump bid or not. God's truth, Katie."

They reached the freeway and squeezed into the southbound traffic. Westward a few hundred yards was the biggest ocean on earth, its enormous blackness generating veils of mist.

"The classifieds are pretty dull stuff these days," he said. "No mystery, no excitement."

She tipped her head back against the headrest. "Too good to last, mahn. Sorry."

"Leetle beet sorry?" he said. "Or *beaucoup?*"

"*Beaucoup.*"

"You know, in a way I'm glad—"

She sat up. "Don't we get off the freeway pretty soon?"

"Next off-ramp." In fact, Dana realized, he had just been directed off Katie's freeway. Very touchy business.

They dipped down an off-ramp and headed for the old highway near the beach, turned south on it through a small beach community, and a half mile farther along reached sea level. He slowed before a collection of buildings huddled behind a rocky breakwater, floodlights illuminating a small surf rolling in under a golden mantle of foam. He parked in the restaurant lot.

Katie sniffed the salty air. "Delicious!" she said.

He opened the car door. In the floodlights, he had his first good look at her. She wore a wine-colored skirt and a frothy pink sweater, her hair falling below her shoulders, unbraided and brushed to a sheen. She gave him a smile that turned another generator on inside him, a real monster this time. He felt as though he was putting out enough voltage to light the entire city of San Diego.

The hostess gave them a table by the windows and lit a candle for them. They could see and hear the little combers crumbling and seeming to ride in on skates. Dana watched Katie glance around, rather shyly, and felt himself sinking. The love he felt for her was excruciating. The candlelight dusted Katie's skin with a sort of golden pollen, illuminated her hair. The candle flame was reflected in her eyes, and the shadows of her cheekbones emphasized the almost Oriental up-tilt of them.

A cocktail waitress came, took one look at them, smiled, told them to enjoy their dinner, and departed. A waitress brought huge plastic menus, and they studied the pictures of seafood.

"Ever eat squid?" Dana asked.

"Squid!" Katie said. "How icky. Do they bring it in a bucket?"

"No, they're cutlets. If you like abalone, you'll love squid. I always have it."

"Make it two. I'm so trusting."

Waiting for their salad, they watched the waves.

"No bad feelings about water?" he asked.

"No. But I won't do that number again!" Then

she quickly dug a scratch pad and pencil from her purse and scrutinized him. "Hold still."

"What's up?"

"I'm going to do you for the annual. Might as well do a practice sketch. I'm doing faculty caricatures for Francis, and he said I could do a few of the flakier students, too."

"Thanks a lot!"

She drew some lines, glancing from him to the pad and back again. He knew she was only putting him off.

"Can I talk while you work?"

"If you don't talk too much."

"There's something I don't understand. How does Marcia get away with this house arrest stuff?"

"She's the warden. What can I do? Run away?"

Dana smiled. "It might work for openers."

"Don't smile. I'm doing you serious."

"I meant it for serious. I don't think she's good for you. What if—"

Katie dropped the pencil and took a breadstick from a tumbler. She buttered the tip and held it to his lips. Feeling foolish, but pleased, he bit off an inch. Then he realized how hard it was to talk seriously with your mouth full. He gulped, took a drink of water, and tried again.

"One thing you could do is talk to Mrs. Allen. Her husband is a lawyer, and maybe—"

Katie buttered the breadstick again and all but

stuck it down his throat, laughing. He turned his head.

"Wait a minute," he said. "I'll bet you didn't know I had two motives in asking you out for dinner. One of them was to talk about your situation at home."

"Is Mrs. Allen writing your stuff? You sound like an amateur shrink."

"I'm trying to be," Dana said, "but you aren't making it any easier. After our big scene the other night, I decided there was a lot I didn't know about you. And as a Concerned Citizen for Katie Norman, I aim to find out."

Katie nibbled a breadstick. He watched her gaze at the floodlit waves, frown, and then glance at him.

"There's really not that much to tell. I'm just your average cheerleader."

"Oh, no! You're not my average anything. You're twelve on a scale of ten. And you're also the only girl I know whose father got custody of her when her parents split up."

Katie frowned at him, her lips pursed, finally pointed a breadstick at him like a pistol and said, "Am I talking to you, or to all your friends, and maybe the whole student body?"

"You're talking to me, in confidence."

"Promise?"

He nodded.

"Okay. Though it's not very interesting. Daddy

was out of the country for a full year, when I was eight or nine. He only came home once. My mom got on diet pills and booze. And she had a lot of friends on big motorcycles. I did the housework, mostly carrying out empties. The neighbors reported us, and the Health Department cordoned off the house and declared it a disaster area. Mom went to a detox center, and they put me in a foster home till my father came back, which was pretty soon."

"Terrible," Dana said.

"They dissolved the marriage and he took a teaching job at State. In about six months he began dragging Marcia home to dinner—she was a student of his. She always brought me something nice, but managed to get me into different clothes because there was a spot on my dress or something, and she'd wash my hands nice and clean and sniff my hair to see if I had washed it. I knew from Day One that she was a fruitcake. But he didn't. And I guess he wanted a mother for me. And darned if I wasn't the flower girl at a backyard wedding in a few months!"

"How old was she?"

"I don't know; nineteen maybe. I think I'd have died of disinfectant poisoning, if she hadn't had Cutepig pretty soon. Then I was fairly safe as long as I didn't touch him."

He took a bite of breadstick, with a lot of butter. He was afraid to comment, afraid not to.

"What did he see in her?" he asked.

"Haven't you noticed? Her form and face. But she didn't marry him to get a nine-year-old daughter—she married him to get a successful husband. I know I got in her way, and I suppose it embarrassed her to tell people, This is my daughter, when she was only twenty or so herself."

"Do you ever see your real mother?" Dana asked.

"She used to send pictures of herself once in a while, usually sitting on a motorcycle with a can of beer in her hand. You know, Kapitan, you can take this roots thing too far sometimes. I'd be better off if I'd never met my mother!"

"Someday," Dana predicted, "Cutepig may be saying the same thing."

"I hope not. But I don't see much of a future for him. She hauls him to the emergency room every time he gets a sniffle. She won't let him grow up. I'm a bad influence on him because I love him, but let him take chances once in a while. Once he fell out of the swing. Oh, brother! If we had a Tower of London, my name would be on the plaque in the garden."

Their dinner came. To his relief she kept talking, faster and faster, as though an ice floe had dissolved in her mind. She said the squid was delicious, smiled, then frowned and talked faster as she ate.

"But that's not the reason I do crazy things.

Will you absolutely keep all this stuff to yourself?" she asked, but went on without waiting for his promise. "The hickies on my neck?" She giggled. "I make them with a piece of surgical tubing! It drives Marcia nuts, because she thinks I'm crawling out the windows or something and having affairs. And the ads . . ."

At last, he thought.

"The ads . . . were because . . . I was jealous of you. Because you know the answers—"

"Me?" he shrugged. "Not many, Katie. Just the easy ones that have landed in my lap. Not like yours. But maybe I could come up with some advice if you ever ask for it."

"I don't know, Kapitan. Pardon me—*garçon.* The ads, hmm. I wanted to rattle your cage, for one thing. Just see what happened. And I wanted to talk to you—I really did want to talk to somebody on the outside, but . . . And I'm not really right for you. You don't know that, maybe, but I do."

"Oh, now, listen—"

"True's God, mahn. I wouldn't be good for you. I'd always be showboating—destructive; bad for you."

"Bad! Aw, Katie. If you knew how my circulation has perked up—"

He reached over and squeezed her hand. She played with her food, but he realized she was just playing for time; she had choked up. But after a moment she took a quick breath and began eating again.

"Like the squid?" he asked.

"Fantastic. —The thing that scares me," she said, "the thing I'm always afraid of—" She took a handkerchief from her purse and blew her nose. "Talk about it later. Maybe. What's the surprise?"

"Did you wear your swimsuit?"

"I'm sitting here in it."

"We're going swimming."

She looked at the ocean, her eyes still damp; but she was smiling. "In *that?*"

"No. In a very private pool. I've got a key. Belongs to a famous editor."

"Whee!" the cheerleader said. "Spirit, drive, ability, oh, you're the best, as I can see!"

In the parking lot he put his arm around her waist and squeezed her against him. His internal organs seemed to melt when she tipped her head against his shoulder for a second. But only a second. Yet he knew his fate was sealed.

29

"Where is this Roman bath?" Katie asked, as they drove south on Old 101. "Are you abducting me, I hope?"

"South Del Mar. Five minutes."

They passed the racetrack and fairgrounds in a slough at the left, speared through the hills of Del Mar in a couple of minutes, and, just where the highway swept down to Torrey Pines Beach, Dana angled left on a side road. The two lanes penetrated a community of condominiums built against a hill. The street became red brick as they entered an area of elegant homes, with street-lights resembling gas lamps.

"Francis lives here," Dana said. "It's called Sea Breeze. . . ."

"Are we going to his house?"

"No. They've got a locked pool for adult residents, and I happen to have the key. I'll park short of it, so it won't give anybody the idea we're swimming up there—"

He parked the Audi against an ivied bank and

peered up at a cnain-link fence. The milky lamps of the pool area were unlighted.

"Green light on Phase One!" he whispered.

He led her to a steel gate, Katie in one arm, the towels in the other. As he fitted the key, she slipped her arm around him. He felt like howling like a wolf. He unlocked the gate and they went through. He had been here as Francis's guest, and knew where everything was, a bathhouse and games area at the left, a pool at the right, with a steaming Jacuzzi in an alcove near the pool. The hot spa caught his eye. What was more relaxing than hot, churning water? She'd be talking like a thousand-dollar parrot in ten minutes.

"Why don't you, um, undress," he suggested, "while I find something to drink?"

" 'Kay!"

He found the drink machine and got two Cokes out of it. Then he stripped down to his trunks, tore off his shoes and socks, glancing her way anxiously as though she might, like a wood nymph, suddenly vanish. Furlong, you will never be so happy again if you live to be a hundred. The most beautiful girl in the world is standing at the edge of the Jacuzzi, awaiting you.

When he carried the drinks and the towels to the Jacuzzi, she was kneeling in the veils of steam at its edge, a small goddess in a dark bikini that was mostly strings. She rose and reached for her drink, looking as excited as he was. A car hummed past without slowing. Sea Breeze was a quiet residential community without through streets. Faint traffic sounds murmured blocks away.

"Let's get in!" she said. "I'm freezing."

She tiptoed down into the hot water, holding his hand. The pool was about eight feet square, bubbling like champagne. Dana followed her, and they sat on submerged benches across from each other. He raised his drink in a toast.

"To Annie-Marie, and her bargain bird basement."

"To her loyal customer."

They drank. The icy Coke slid down his throat like a sword. "You were saying, 'The thing I'm scared of,' when we left the restaurant," he reminded her.

"Was I? I don't remember."

"Come on, Katie. Don't tease."

She sipped, then blew a solemn bass note across the neck of the bottle. "Funny farms," she said.

"What?"

"Just kidding."

"No, you weren't. You mean—you don't like shrinks?"

"Or authority figures."

"Like Marcia?"

"Like a lot of people."

"Ever think," he asked, "of going to a boarding

school? It would get you out of Marcia's custody."

"But what about Cutepig? I couldn't live without him."

"Know why you need him so much?" Dana said. "He's about all you've got. In a boarding school, you'd have friends, and visitors—me—and no witch to harass you."

Katie stood up. Her bosom bobbled just above the level of the water. It must be hard for male psychiatrists, he thought, with beautiful patients, to keep their minds on their work. She was bouncing on the balls of her feet and he could not keep his eyes off her breasts. It was an effort to keep his hands off them.

"Okay, I've thought about it," she said. "But there are too many problems."

"More than at home?"

She lay on her back to float in the steam and swirling water. He watched her. She was eluding him, he realized. But he had made progress. He called to her.

"What?" she said.

"On your feet. Talk to me."

She turned over and stood up, started jumping again and then looked down at herself, and crouched suddenly in the water. "Eek!" she said.

An object brushed his leg, slithered up his thigh. A Jacuzzi viper? He trapped it and held up a wisp of fabric. Katie squealed.

"That's mine! Give it to me."

He held it up and saw that it was a scrap of blue nylon with strings, and a metal clasp. Folded up, it could have been fitted inside a walnut shell; but it happened to be her bikini top! An excitement like a charge of electricity roared through him, a strong blend of sexual force, discovery, and the suspicion that he was being teased.

"Dana!" Katie said, her hands over her bosom. "You fiend. Give it back."

He was *sure* she had not lost it. She had unhooked something. "Finders keepers," he said.

"You animal!" Katie hissed. "Come on—don't make me write my congressperson."

"Dear Senator Blah," Dana teased. "My bra is being held hostage by a terrorist. The man who has it wants two kisses."

"One kiss," she sighed.

"Two," he insisted.

She grabbed, but he held it behind him. She was a bare two feet from him now, her hands on her hips; it was clear to him that he was being teased, and that she had better than a centerfold figure.

"Vun kiss," he said. "Ve meet your demands."

She laughed, came closer, and pushed her face toward him, with her eyes squeezed shut. Dana tossed the bikini top on the cement and pulled her to him. She did not resist, and he caught her in his arms, dizzy with desire, rashness, and some anxiety about what he was doing. He kissed her, and when she tried to push away, held her against him and ran a hand up to her breast.

She suddenly tore loose, laughing, and struggled onto the cement. As she started to crawl away, he floundered after her, caught her by an ankle, and she sprawled, laughing. He crawled up and threw his arm across her shoulders, kissing her cheek.

"Katie!" he whispered.

She did not respond, even stir, and he turned her face so that he could see it; and at last he knew that she was crying. Her features were contorted. She was sobbing.

"Katie—?" he whispered, shocked. "What's wrong? I thought—"

"You thought you'd bought me—?" She crawled away, found her bra, and walked off to put it on.

"Katie, please—! Oh, dammit, listen—"

He found the towels, handed her one and she yanked it away and walked toward her clothing, heaped on a bench near the fence.

Miserably, Dana dried off and dressed. I don't believe this! he thought. She did it on purpose. The clasp had not appeared broken. And although he had never undressed a girl, he felt sure a bra did not fall off that easily.

When he was dressed, he went over and found her huddled on the bench, shivering, her hair in strings. "Please, Katie," he said. "Can't I explain? I thought—"

"Oh, damn," she said. "Damn, damn—"

"I'm sorry."

"Oh, fine, it's alright, then." She got up quickly and ran toward the gate. Dana strode after her.

"I thought you were teasing me. It wouldn't be the first time a girl—"

She looked at him in disgust. "Thank you, Kapitan," she said. "I had sex hygiene, too. I know what animals we are. So forget it and take me home. You got to play your big scene. The one where you showed me what you love about me."

He tried to open the car door for her, but she slapped his hand down and got in by herself.

She never uttered one word all the way home.

He watched her slip through the front door, and then saw a light go on in a room at the back of the house.

Oh, my God, he thought.

Should I wake up Marcia? Will she try anything again?

He drove off a few hundred yards and stopped, turned the lights off, and pondered. He had driven her like a truck, and she was a formula racing car.

Or was she merely making sure he appreciated her by this performance?

He tried to believe it. There was nothing else to

hang onto. Tomorrow he would find her, and probably she would have changed moods, like changing a blouse, and he could make things right.

30

Katie usually arrived early, so Dana parked his moped fifteen minutes before first-period biology in order to be there to welcome her when the red Porsche whirled into the parking lot. The morning was dark and cold, a wind blowing in off the ocean. Students climbed the steps, friends speaking to him as he sat on the rail. He gave them a pallid grin. Every thirty or forty seconds he consulted his watch, tormented by a growing dread as the ant-trail of students dwindled. He had come here buoyed somewhat by the teaser theory, the corollary of which was that after she had let him suffer awhile, she would forgive him.

But ten minutes after the bells rang, he realized the rules had been changed. She was not coming. He slouched off to biology, crucified by the dangers of the situation. That she had taken pills again; run away; been caught coming in by Marcia and confined to quarters.

He sat half-conscious in his place.

". . . Furlong?"

Mr. Lockwood was speaking to him. The question had failed to penetrate the mud of his gloom; he had not heard the question. "I'm sorry—?" he said.

Lunkhead, that old brown-shirted, butch-tonsured phony, stood with the textbook in his hand, grinning. "Amphibians, Furlong," he said. "What does the name mean?"

Dana glanced toward Paul, who signaled "two," with his fingers. "Um, living on land and water?" he hazarded.

"Somebody else, who's read the lesson?" the teacher said, and picked a girl, naturally.

"Literally, it means having two lives."

"Right. Run that through Mr. Burroughs' little invention, Furlong, which I see you forgot to pin to your belt this morning."

"My calculator?" Dana said, rousing gamely to the challenge.

"Isn't that what you usually wear on your belt?"

"Yes, but the calculator wasn't invented by Burroughs," Dana said.

Lunkhead chortled. "Mr. Burroughs got his patent in 1888. It wasn't Texas Instruments, in 1975, as you may have thought."

"No, I thought it was Pascal, in the seventeenth century," Dana said.

"Wrong! Dead wrong! Pascal was a philosopher-mathematician—"

"And a lot of other things," Dana said, "and if you'll look it up in the book, you'll see that he invented an adding machine, which another Frenchman improved into a calculator. But I think Pascal is regarded as the father of the calculator."

"I'll tell you what," the teacher said. "You can do a little paper on that subject, due Monday. No credit, but a lot of education."

Dana shrugged. Lunkhead appeared puzzled at his lack of zest for a debate.

He kept praying she would show up late, but the chair beside him remained ominously empty. He dissected a frog with a different lab partner, made the notes, and let the girl do the drawings and labelings. They were crude and almost unrecognizable, unlike Katie's precise little pictures.

When the bell rang he was out the door and down the labyrinth to Amanda Allen's room.

Her second-period students were just shuffling in as he slipped up beside her desk. He thought she looked tight-lipped and preoccupied. "Yes?" she said.

Dana glanced out over the room, lowered his voice, and asked, "Do you have Katie this period?"

"Yes."

"Well, I don't think she's here today. She wasn't in biology. I'd better talk to you, Mrs. Allen. Can I meet you here during the lunch hour?"

"Of course. I want to talk to you, too."

"What about?"

"A telephone call we had about midnight last night. My husband answered, but no one spoke. He had the impression it was made from a pay phone on the street somewhere."

"You just got caught in the tender trap," Paul said, in the cafeteria, as Dana, appetiteless, played with a helping of tamale pie.

"You're learning about girls," Francis said. "Of *course* she did it on purpose. By the way, may I have the pool key back?"

"Sorry." Dana produced it. "Thanks."

"Try it again some time. She'll come around."

Dana drank some water and swished it through his teeth, hating to show up for an important conference with food on his incisors; then he darted off.

Mrs. Allen was just approaching her room as he hurried up from the other direction. He searched her face for encouragement, but she looked, if anything, even more glum than before. She went in, motioned him to a chair near her desk, sat down, and dropped her purse in a drawer.

"I managed to reach her stepmother," she said. "She hadn't left for work yet. No car. She was waiting for a rental to arrive."

"How come?" Dana asked.

"Katie borrowed her car last night and took off."

Dana slid down in the seat. "Oh, man. Oh, man! Did she wreck it?"

"No, she hasn't reported in. Could her disappearance be related to anything that happened last night?"

Dana hooked his hands under his belt and stared at his shoes. "It could be. It certainly could," he admitted. "I came on like a beast, she said. I swear, Mrs. Allen, I thought I'd been, you know, invited! I mean—"

The teacher shook her head. "Oh, Dana. I hated to warn you, but maybe I should have. A lot of girls will tease that way. But a girl like Katie might overdo it, get an overreaction from the boy, and then go bananas when he started undressing her. Is that more or less what happened?"

"More or less."

"I see. Well, did you learn anything about her state of mind before you made a beast of yourself?"

"Quite a bit," Dana said, eager to absolve himself. He related the conversation at dinner, and Katie's seeming relief in letting off steam, not to mention letting him put his arm around her.

"Well, so then I let her out at her place, and she ran inside."

"Then she took the car, drove off, and called my house," said Mrs. Allen.

"Why didn't she talk?" Dana asked.

"Why do disturbed people do a lot of things? I think she wants to stay in touch, although she's in a pretty precarious condition. The fact that she's already had a couple of auto accidents, of course, is the really worrisome factor. But I think she'll talk to us, eventually. She'll probably call you, and maybe you can get her to talk. Actually, we've had several of these mysterious calls over the last few weeks. I think she's been sending up signals almost since she came to Santo Tomas."

Dana hunched forward and rested his elbows on his knees.

"Don't sit that way," Mrs. Allen said. "You look like a poster for suicide prevention. Think and act positively. God knows we're not going to get any help from her stepmother, so it's up to us."

"Has she called the police?"

"No. And *I* can't, of course, because it's not my car. I asked her to, because the main thing is to get Katie back. But she says the girl is just joyriding around and she'll come back and face the music when she feels like it."

"What about her father? Can we get in touch with him?"

"She says she doesn't know where he's staying. A likely story. I'll check with the educators' association. She is deliberately letting Katie get away with it, hoping she'll disgrace or injure herself. I will poison that woman if I ever get her over here again."

The cold wind made his eyes water as he rode home after school. Where would I go, he wondered, if I wanted to get away from everybody?

Probably down to Baja, if I could pass for eighteen at the border crossing. But she couldn't. If I got turned back, I'd probably look for a beach to hang around for a couple of days. Eat hamburgers, sleep in the car. But he realized he could not think like Katie, because he did not feel remotely like Katie. What he felt like was belting a brick wall with his fist, to punish himself for his stupidity.

Turning into his street, he considered more useful alternatives.

Try to list every clue she ever gave him as to where she might go. What kind of scenery did she like? Beaches, mountains, desert? Or just to drive, maybe. They had had a family friend once who took off driving every Friday night, headed for some exciting spot like Fresno, Needles, Death Valley, and kept track of the gas she used and where she ate; turned around then and drove home; and, later, bored you with an account of her mileage and elapsed time.

But she was not at all like Katie. She was a clod. Katie was . . .

The telephone was shrilling as he walked into the house.

31

He heard Wendy's voice in the kitchen, saying, "Hello? Hello?"

When he ran in, she was holding the telephone receiver in her hand. "I ran in, but when I answered nobody said anything," she reported indignantly.

"Let me have it," Dana said. "And listen—*please* go to your bedroom for a few minutes, will you? Please?"

She looked at him with her mouth slightly open; she wasn't really stupid, it was just that her nose stopped up at times. Then she shrugged and walked away.

"Hello."

Saying that, he lowered himself into a kitchen chair. He heard a very faint ringing, and then a car swishing past; stopping; starting up.

"Katie, it's Dana! Where are you?"

Another silence; another car, groaning to a stop in the background, then starting up with a snoring sound.

"Why won't you talk?"

No reply.

"Amanda called your home and talked to Marcia. She hasn't told the police, so nothing's going to happen to you. But I've got something to say to you. It has nothing to do with your home, just with us. Are you ready for this?"

He heard another car and another. Apparently the first made a boulevard stop, the other pulled on by without slowing. How could that be? He waited until there was no traffic noise, then said, "I love you, Katie. That's all I was trying to say last night. I just got carried away."

He heard a sound, a vocable without meaning. Then silence, followed by the dial tone. She had hung up.

He dialed Mrs. Allen's number, but she was not home yet.

One of his problems was that he was uncomfortable with secrets. They burned in him like excess stomach acid.

He went to Wendy's open door and said, looking in at her as she innocently brushed her hair, "Did you listen?"

"Well—sure. What do you think I am?"

"If you come outside, I'll tell you something."

He carried the telephone outside and placed it on a wrought-iron table beside a chair. He needed to see and hear the birds doing their uncomplicated things while this nightmare went on.

"Yeah?" she said. She blew her nose on a tissue.

"Well, that girl I told you about—it was her on the phone."

"What's she trying to prove?"

"God, I wish I knew! We had a disagreement last night, and she borrowed her stepmother's Porsche when she got home, and left."

"What's she going to do?"

"Try to scare everybody, I guess." He was tapping both feet on the cement, rapid-fire.

"Is she running away?"

"She's already run away, Wendy. That's the problem. I wonder if a sixteen-year-old can check in at a motel?"

"Why won't she talk? That's dumb."

"She wants help, but can't ask for it. She's—well, she's suicidal."

"Really?" Wendy wrinkled her nose. "Does she act strange?"

"No. Mrs. Allen says she wants me to help her, but can't let me."

The telephone rang again. Dana grabbed at it.

"Dana, this is Amanda Allen," the teacher's calm voice said. "Have you heard from her?"

"Yes, but she didn't say anything. I heard the same traffic sounds your husband heard. There must be a boulevard stop where she calls, because I could hear cars stopping and starting."

"Stay in there, Dana. I managed to reach her father, in Honolulu. He's taking a plane home tonight. He admits he's been worried about Katie for some time, and he's furious with Marcia, to put it mildly. When Katie does talk, try to keep her talking, about anything. If you get a chance to give her any advice, you might mention the fact that there are always alternatives to suicide."

"Like what?"

"Well, she probably took some money with her, and she loves to paint. How about going to the desert, staying at a motel, and painting out her anxieties? Maybe she'll feel different after some time alone. Or she could insist that her father put her in a boarding school. Or dye her hair red. There are so many things she could do, but the only decision she'd be stuck with is suicide."

Wendy drifted into the family room just after he hung up. "Where's Mom?" Dana asked her.

"She was having her hair done, and then she was going shopping, and she's meeting Dad for dinner. What are we having?"

"Hamburgers, if I feel like cooking. Peanut butter out of the jar, if I don't."

He carried the telephone back to the patio so he could reach it quickly while he worked with the birds. He hung a couple of palm fronds in lovebird aviaries, remembering the call in his mind. Light traffic, but no trucks. There had been too much traffic for the Old Stage Road area, where she lived, so she wasn't making the calls from home, which was a possibility now that Marcia had left. On the other hand, the traffic had been far too light for the city. She had called from a pay phone at a queer boulevard stop where some cars stopped and others did not. Why didn't all traffic stop, or none?

Dusk settled like smoke, then darkness closed in. Was she eating in some roadside joint? Was she driving farther and farther away? Would a call come sometime tonight from Mrs. Allen? "Dana, I'm sorry to have to tell you this, but I just heard from a hospital in Los Angeles . . ."

He got hamburger makings out of the refrigerator and shaped the meat patties. He placed them in the frying pan—and jumped as the telephone went off like a land mine. He faced it with wild eyes, then wiped the grease from his hands with a paper towel (wondering why it mattered?) and grabbed the handset.

"Hello!"

It could have been anybody, but he knew it was Katie again. When he heard the vacant line sounds, he let himself onto a chair and listened. Then, fighting for calmness, he said:

"This is Dana. Katie?"

A car hummed by without stopping.

"Katie, please listen. Mrs. Allen called Honolulu and managed to reach your father. He's coming home, and he's plenty mad at Marcia. *You're* not in trouble, baby, but *she's* going to be when he asks her why she didn't tell him about the pills thing. You're very important to him. To all of us, Katie."

This time he heard sounds that told him she was crying. "So why don't you drive to my place?" he asked. "And we'll go to Mrs. Allen's, and talk all night if you want. You've been bottling it up too long, trying to work it out yourself. It can't be done. What did you do last night?"

More of the small noises that told him only that she was there.

"Know what I'd do?" he said. "I'd go to Baja and camp on the beach. I've camped it with Paul and some other guys, and it's really great. There are tide pools that are unbelievable, sea anemones a foot across. But the water is icy. Isn't that odd?"

". . . Hemingway!" she sobbed.

"Hemingway, Katie, was a sick man," Dana said. "He wasn't emotionally disturbed, like you—he was sick. Most of these people you've been writing essays about were sick people. There's nothing much wrong with you that getting away from Marcia wouldn't cure. It's worth trying. And I'll bet the first thing your father does when he gets home—"

The line emptied like a kitchen sink, and a young woman's voice said, "Deposit thirty-five cents for another three minutes, please."

"You can charge it to this number, operator," Dana said quickly. But the coins were already chiming in that pay phone thirty-five cents away. In what direction? He started to ask where the call was coming from, but feared Katie might panic and run. But then he had a better idea.

"If we talk overtime, operator, just charge it to this number."

"Alright, sir."

"Katie? Quit thinking about famous suicides, and think about yourself. Maybe all you need is a total break from the grind. Got any money with you?"

"A little," she said.

"Then drive somewhere nice and do a painting! The weather ought to be fantastic over in the Borrego Desert. Hour's drive. Forget everything else. Get a motel room. But call me, for Pete's sake, so I won't be worrying."

There was no reply. Cars passed, some stopping, some not. Dana, for some reason, felt slightly encouraged.

"Listen, Katie, I'll make you a bet. I'll bet you a lovebird that if you stay where you are, you'll see me inside of an hour. You said I could problem-solve and all that. So have a hamburger, if there's a restaurant near where you are. But don't run, or the bet's off. Sit tight and wait for Das Kapitan."

She hung up, and he winced, having no idea whether things were better or worse. The dial tone buzzed. He dialed the operator quickly.

"I need the charges on a toll call that was billed to this number just now. Can you give it to me right away? I'd like to know the number it was made from, too."

He heard papers shuffling, then the operator saying, "Seven-four-two, six-nine hundred."

"Where is that, operator?"

"Pauma Valley."

"Thank you.

He smacked the tabletop with both palms, and laughed in glee. "I got it, I got it!" he yelled.

Wendy glided in. "What are you going to do?"

"Listen! Call Amanda Allen for me, will you? Her number is written down right here. Tell her what you heard. I've got to take off. Damn, both cars are gone, I'll have to ride the moped. Oh, well, there's no freeway between there and here, so it won't be a problem."

"Where's Pauma Valley?"

"At the foot of the Palomar Observatory grade."

32

Dana's moped sang through the hills, past the turnoff to Bill St. John's aviaries, over the two-lane road to the mountains. At San Marcos there was a freeway link to Escondido, but he had to stay on the winding highway as it threaded through brushy hills and low passes.

He pictured the Pauma Valley road at the foot of the Palomar grade, remembering a three-way intersection with a triangular traffic island in the middle. Traffic coming from the north hit the grade without stopping; cars arriving from the coast had to stop. So that accounted for the fact that some cars made a stop, and some did not.

The fact that there was very little life at the summit, only a campground and a few stores, explained the absence of truck traffic. It was still early spring up there—nearly six thousand feet higher than at the base of the mountains—and that made the traffic still lighter. It was eight-thirty when he passed Escondido, buzzing along the northern edge of the long narrow valley, which meant there would be still less traffic when he arrived.

A few insects struck the visor of his helmet. There were horses in fields to the right, a few crops to the left. Beyond the valley the road climbed a little, then dropped down to Valley Center, a farm crossroads with a few stores.

Now he was on the last ten-minute leg of the trip. He had been on the road hardly a half hour. What was he going to say to her? He had already given her his best shots.

Where, precisely, had she telephoned from?

Well, there was a miniature savings-and-loan office tucked into the oaks at the intersection. He recalled a tiny parking lot, but could not remember whether there was a telephone booth.

Otherwise, the nearest telephone booth was a couple of hundred feet up the road, at the Stage Stop, a grocery store and real estate office. He definitely remembered a telephone there. But could you hear cars halting, from the Stage Stop?

Beyond Valley Center it was little farms, a vineyard, everything hidden in cold darkness. Country mailboxes askew along the road. Then some orange groves, jungles of sprawly avocado trees in ominous masses, and dark groves of huge old lemon trees. Now and then he saw the mountain, an enormous bulk discernible only because it blotted out the starry sky. The air was very clear out here—

Suddenly he realized he was in the stretch! Olive trees and sycamores loomed on one side, a big old lemon grove on the other. And just ahead he saw taillights, as a car made a boulevard stop. He looked over the dark panorama . . . the three-way intersection with its traffic island . . . old-fashioned power lines like cobwebs . . . a burned-out adobe behind olive trees on the left . . . the savings-and-loan with its little parking lot at the right of the stop.

He saw a telephone booth under a sycamore tree in the lot. Beside it a small car was parked. His headlight picked it up. *Red!* Hot dog!

But as he swung into the lot, an engine snarled, the lights went on in the car, and gravel spat. She was going to run! But how had she known? —well, the single headlight, of course. If he had had a car to drive, she wouldn't have known it was he until he had her.

The car headed like a scalded cat up the two-lane road climbing the grade. He putt-putted doggedly after the little red sports car. She in a Porsche and he on a moped! It would go in Guinness if he ever caught her. Her taillights were out of sight in twenty seconds. She was traveling fast, and he was doing his maximum thirty uphill.

Shall I try to telephone ahead? Call the restaurant at the top, get them to grab her? It all seemed too vague; he didn't have the restaurant's name anyway—a health food place—probably closed at this decent Christian hour.

He saw her lights again. She must have pulled over to let him catch up. But as soon as his one-eyed steed came in view, she raced on up the grade. In a short time she vanished once more. There was a fragrance of sage and oily pesticides. Then he saw headlights coming. Had she turned around? But they were too wide-set for a sports car. It was a van that passed him, heading west.

The next time he saw her was on a horseshoe turn. She had slowed on the high side of the curve, heading south; he was below, heading north into the turn. She sped off. Hopeless, hopeless!

But it gave him an idea.

He remembered a straight stretch not far above. There were several such runs before the road buckled and went all to hell for the steeper climb. He felt sure she would slow down to let him close up—a teaser to the finish!

He bulled along like a furious bumblebee, stealing unnerving glimpses of precipitous drops at the left, then at the right. No safety rails on this hairpin grade. Beside the road grew oaks, brush, and cedars. The road straightened suddenly, with loose earth borders on each side. He switched off his headlight. If he couldn't overtake her, he might get close enough at least for some strategy.

He saw twin ruby lights on the right-hand

parking strip. She was waiting. He bent low over the cowling, keeping his eyes on her, steering by dead reckoning. No lights, no moon. The taillights enlarged as he closed in. Then they dimmed, and he knew she had taken her foot off the brake pedal, preparing to blast off again.

Dana switched on his headlight, waited five seconds, then performed a couple of crazy swerves, cut suddenly into the dirt and laid the moped over in a slide. He cut the engine and let the headlight beam crisscross the ground, wildly. Then he sprawled in the light. For still more drama, he pulled off his helmet and let it roll away.

Man down! Hurt bad!

He could hear the Porsche whining. Would she notice his lights go awry? See the bike on the ground, the injured rider? The Porsche kept pulling away, the lights dwindling. Then the engine sounds ceased and brakelights burned. He lay still. The ground was warmer than the air. He could hear his engine snapping like a beetle as it cooled, smelled the sugary chaparral.

Headlights swiveled around, swept the brush and boulders, flooded the road, and the Porsche was coming back!

As it slowed across the blacktop from him, he rolled onto his back and let one arm fall limply on the ground. He heard a girl's cry. A brake rasped, the door opened, and Katie was running across the road toward him, screaming *"Dana!"* She was still wearing the dark-red dress and pink sweater. She knelt in the earth beside him, her palms on his cheeks as she peered into his face.

"Dana! Oh, God! Please—"

". . . Katie?" he whispered.

"Yes! Can you move? You aren't paralyzed?"

Dana put his hand to his head. "Just a little groggy."

"Can you move your legs?"

He moved them, play-acted sitting up with difficulty. She helped him, pulling at his arm, getting in his way, weeping.

"Now you know how *I* felt," he said soberly. "You'd have been responsible if I'd broken my neck."

She sat on the ground beside him. "You're alright!" she said. "You just did that . . ."

"St. Dana never fails," he said. "Wait here, my child. Bless you."

He got up and went to park her car farther off the road. She continued to sit by his moped, sobbing. He moved the bike into the brush, hiding it in a thicket of scrub oak.

He sat by her and took her hand. It was limp. He gave her his handkerchief, and she blew her nose. "You wouldn't want a *dumb* boyfriend, would you?" he said. "I got you stopped, right? And tomorrow we'll get you started."

"There's a card—" she sniffled. "On the passenger's seat. Will you get it?"

"A card?"

"A business card."

He found it by the dashlight, a crumpled business card lying on the leather seat. In the light he read it.

Beth Lasser, Ph.D.

Clinical Psychologist.

He carried it back and gave it to her. "No—keep it for me," she said. "I don't want to lose it. Mrs. Allen gave it to me. I started to call the lady, but I couldn't seem to do it."

"You'll have to. Where do you want to stay tonight? My place or Mrs. Allen's?"

"Mrs. Allen's, I guess."

"I'll call her from the foot of the grade. She's probably going crazy worrying about you. Your father, too—he's on the plane right now. Ready?" he asked her.

"Okay."

They crossed the road to the car, his arm supporting her She let him open the car door for her and got in, then tipped her head back against the headrest with a sigh. Dana hurried around to the driver's side. He slid in quickly, but studied the diagram on the gearshift knob before starting the car. It was hardly the time to back into the ditch by accident. Katie uttered a tired giggle.

"So organized," she murmured.

Dana patted her hand. He started the engine

and drove off. Two minutes later, when he pulled suddenly into the parking lot from which she had made her calls, she sat up quickly, as if coming out of a dream. "Where are we?"

"You've got a telephone call to make, baby," Dana said. "Dr. Lasser. Remember?"

She shook her head. "Oh, no! No, Dana," she pleaded. "I'm so tired. I couldn't explain it to anybody. . . . You don't realize how—how much—"

Dana pried her limp hand open and pressed a dime onto her palm. "Put this in the slot. Here's her card. Call her collect and let her do the talking."

Protesting feebly, she let him lead her to the booth. In the glassed-in cabin, she stood with her head down for a while, then closed the door to turn the light on, and looked at the card. Then she placed the coin in the slot, and he heard it *ding*. A long pause—a car passed—but at last he heard her say, in a faint voice, "This is Katie Norman, Dr. Lasser. Mrs. Allen's . . . student . . ."

Dana stood with his hands in his pockets, sniffing the lemon blossoms and feeling the strain easing out of his body. He had not realized he was so tense. Every now and then she would say, "yes," or "no." Finally she came out and stood close to him, in silence.

"Hungry?" he asked her.

"Starved. I haven't had anything to eat since

the squid." She started giggling, and he was afraid she would become hysterical, but she stopped, sighed, and leaned gainst him.

"We'll pig out on hamburgers in Escondido," Dana said. "Hop in."

In Escondido they found a drive-in and ate hamburgers and shakes in the car, listening to a sentimental-music station on the car radio. Katie became very silent halfway through the second hamburger, and he saw that she was asleep, her mouth open and her head tipped back. She did not waken even when he started the car, and he drove slowly from the town and down a country highway toward the coast, holding her hand and smiling to himself, tipsy with tenderness and contentment.